PROOFS AND THREE PARABLES

by the same author

fiction

ANNO DOMINI

THE PORTAGE TO SAN CRISTOBAL

non-fiction

THE DEATH OF TRAGEDY

IN BLUEBEARD'S CASTLE: SOME NOTES TOWARDS
THE RE-DEFINITION OF CULTURE

LANGUAGE AND SILENCE

REAL PRESENCES:
IS THERE ANYTHING IN WHAT WE SAY?

TOLSTOY OR DOSTOEVSKY:
AN ESSAY IN CONTRAST

GEORGE STEINER

PROOFS
and Three Parables

faber and faber
LONDON · BOSTON

This collection first published in 1992
by Faber and Faber Limited
3 Queen Square London WC1N 3AU

Photoset by Parker Typesetting Service, Leicester
Printed in England by Clays Ltd, St Ives plc

These stories were first published in *Granta*

A CIP record for this book
is available from the British Library

ISBN 0-571-16621-0

2 4 6 8 10 9 7 5 3 1

for Jeanne and Daniel Singer

Contents

PROOFS (1991), 1

DESERT ISLAND DISCS (1986), 77

NOËL, NOËL (1989), 89

CONVERSATION PIECE (1985), 99

These fictions first appeared in *Granta*. They owe much to Bill Buford's impassioned eye for detail and gusto for concision.

G.S.

PROOFS

Now the burn seemed to smart behind his eyes.

Thirty years and more a master of his craft. The quickest, most accurate of proof-readers and correctors in the whole city, perhaps in the province. Working every night, and throughout the night. So that the legal records, deeds of sale, notifications of public finance, contracts, quotations on the bourse, would appear in the morning, flawless, exact to the decimal point. He had not rival in the arts of scruple. They gave him the smallest print to check, the longest columns of figures to justify, the interminable catalogues of lost and found objects to be auctioned for the post-office and public transport. His proof-readings of the bi-annual telephone directory, of electoral and census rolls, of municipal minutes, were legend. Printing works, the public record office, the courts of law vied for his labours.

But now the sensation of burning, just behind his eyes, felt sharper.

A lifetime inhaling the tang of fresh ink, of lead warm to the touch. The linoleum in his cubicle, his sanctum of the unerring, shook to the beat of the presses. Rotogravure, linotype, electronic type-casting, photo-engraving – he had seen them all. He had outwitted the imperfection, the recursive bugs, the clotted snarls and gremlin upsets of each technique. He knew the provenance, weight, water-mark, fibre-content, resistance to ink-roller and hot metal of diverse papers by the antennae in his thumb. As he knew the impatient awe of the sub-editor, stockmarket messenger, auctioneer, bank-clerk, notary public poised at the door of his cell, waiting for the discrete, singular check-mark, his as famous as the colophon of a renowned designer or the

3

signature of a great artist. The incision of his pencil or ballpoint at the extreme right-hand bottom corner of the page signifying: *nihil obstat*, this text is ready, error-free, sanctified by precision. Let it be printed, published, franked, mailed to reader or tax-payer, to client or dealer, to litigant or advocate. There to order the world as only print can. Codex, pandect, register, the pamphlet or the tome. Now check-marked. His mark, sometimes before the ink was entirely dry. Legendary as is all perfection.

And with the burn, like a thread of smoke, a blur.

He who had never known the weariness of other proof-readers. Their migraines. Their losses of concentration and trembling fingers. The law-students and unemployed lawyers who read proofs for libel in the late evening or early morning stared at him blear-eyed and envious. The firm in charge of printing lists of share-holders for market flotations had, in irked humour, offered a prize for anyone who could spot an error, be it a false initial, in his work. The bottle of champagne remained uncollected. He had heard a tale of proof-readers in another country, men no more schooled than he was, who had corrected the formal arguments in an august work of mathematical logic simply because they observed irregularities in the prescribed system of symbolic and algebraic notations. The story filled him with pride. Once an antique dealer, waiting for his catalogue of manuscripts, autographs and curiosa to be proof-read, had recounted a strange story of a printing error that transmuted the lines of a paltry Elizabethan poet into inviolate gold. Some vagabond had written banalities of a lady whose hair was greying, from whose hair a former brightness had fallen – of which cliché a hurried printer had made the words 'a brightness falls from the air'. To those for whom the language lives, the poetaster was now immortal. He both

4

cherished and hated that anecdote. It made him feel strangely ill like the smell of sex in his younger years. Any erratum is a final untruth.

He rubbed his eyes. The forbidden, hitherto unnecessary gesture. The savour of ink and cigarette ash on the back of his hands was, momentarily, pungent. Behind and below him the presses were hammering.

It was the instant he loved best, almost childishly. At the ebb of night when he restored the finely sharpened pencils to their case, the frayed one in which his father had kept his straight-edged razors, and replaced the congeries of erasers, corrector-fluids and masking-tape in the right-hand drawer, then switched off the light. After which he locked the door to his cubicle and touched his cap, in discrete valediction, to the printers, messengers and packers on the loud floor below. Next he emerged through the small heavy door into first light. Into the first breath of the coming day. The thermos under his arm was now empty. Also the sandwich-bag, unless the cadence of the night's deadlines had been too pressing. If empty, he dropped it in the bin at the corner. He hated litter. Waste paper struck him as the very waste of waste. A devastation. At times, if the winds blew a piece towards his feet, he would pick it up, smooth it, read closely and make any correction needed. Then he would deposit it in the garbage receptacle, feeling obscurely rewarded and saddened. Any witness to this rite would have thought him deranged. But he did not cut a conspicuous figure.

He stood, waiting for morning to print shadows on the warehouse roof. There paper was stacked in leviathan rolls, waiting for the delivery trucks and messengers' mopeds to bark into life. He felt the cool of dawn on his skin. The sheer mad wonder of sunrise, even when it was veiled or rain-swept. Even when it was little more than a lost sheen behind the frequent fogs. He turned slightly eastward, to the native place of morning. Then down the metal steps, towards the square and the tram which would take him home.

[2]

He was thoroughly familiar to the tram-drivers and ticket-inspectors on their milk-run. Among themselves they called him Owl. Not only because of his night-job and of the ruffled, blinking mien with which he mounted the street-car platform, but for the way in which, his frayed pea-green muffler wound around his thin neck, he perched immediately behind the conductor, closely observant. Exact craft fascinated and consoled him. He took renewed pleasure each morning in the driver's measured touch of the starting lever, in the flick he gave the brake-handle, in the fine gauging which seemed to guide the exact speed at which he took the tight clanging curve that led into Via Grande. In the late afternoon or early evening, in turn, when journeying back to work, he savoured the adjustments conductors made to balance their cars when they were thronged, when more and more passengers, homeward bound, elbowed their way through the automatic doors. Eyes shut, he could, according to the lurch of the tram and the particular sound of the grinding gears and overhead wires, tell unerringly where he was, and at which of the eleven stops between Santa Lucia and the printing works the car was whining to a halt. Sometimes he and the inspector exchanged views. But he was not spendthrift of words. There had been too many through the night; there would be too many more during the night ahead, miniscule, tightly aligned, prodigal of mistakes.

Why converse when he could scan the city as it passed? He

knew his transit by heart. Façade by façade, street-corner by street-corner, each junction inwardly mapped. He knew the cobblestones which led down an alley from Piazza Borromeo to the glass-blowing manufacture in which his father had had his lungs shredded by searing dust (compensation had been refused). As the tram rattled on, he could peruse the house-fronts, the names over the shops. At the merest glance. The texts changed. Buildings were torn down and remade. He had seen small archipelagos of green tarred over and flower-beds uprooted. A garage now stood where there had been the malodorous, choked Fountain of the Three Masks. To be noted most alertly was the coming and going of placards, billboards, national, regional and civic notices, graffiti, which his eyes had taken in untiringly as the tram slowed or accelerated.

The memory of the marmoreal and Augustan placards of triumph, that man on his white horse, his chins mountainous, remained heavy inside him. He could visualize still the letters in flame-red on the call-up notices, on the decrees of rejoicing or retribution. Unforgettable were the ochre and black – the brazen type-face of the roll of hostages executed in vengeance. After the liberation came the plethora of election posters with their sheaves of grain, Phrygian caps, roosters crowing to azure skies, hammers and sickles, and laurelled women with bounding children at their heels. A flaking, perpetually changing palimpsest which he had to leaf through at speed as the tram churned by. With the raucous years, posters had been glued on posters, promise on promise, edicts of fiscal reform preceding edicts, each in turn scissored by the winds that came from the nearby mountains in the blue of late September, then discoloured and made soggy refuse by the winter rains.

Now the placards and inscriptions were different. They

proclaimed lagoons, platinum beaches, palmy cruises on the never never. Overnight deities of pop beckoned. Hamburgers house-high, softly ebullient with the blood-tide of ketchup. There flashed past the leather twist of the horror-film. Everywhere bodies shone bronzed yet ethereal. A world so neon-lit, so thrustingly on offer that it demanded to be viewed through those sunglasses, harlequinned and dolphin-tailed. The fonts, the leading, the designs sickened him. Brutal machine-work. He seemed to hear the pulping of silent forests being pounded to dust so as to produce the lettering used on lavatory tiles. Nevertheless, he could not turn away. On each tram journey he read on, mesmerized.

As he neared home, the shops were opening. His needs were few and pedantically habitual. He drank his coffee under the arcades on Liberation Square. Then bought his bread in one of the very few small bakeries left in the district. He had weaknesses: for sardines lightly grilled, for anchovies from the Balearic Islands (the western Mediterranean having become, as headlines proclaimed, a 'cesspit'). He chose his cheeses with deliberation. The narrow, cavernous shop stayed cool even in the weeks of white heat. He favoured goat-cheese and, especially, a gritty variety from the interior of Sardinia. On occasion, he lingered over the fruit and vegetable stalls. They had been grey and fibrous at the end of war and for some time after. Now they beckoned, chromatic and opulent as a Persian carpet. Offering plump asparagus, pink grapefruit, blood-oranges, egg-plant, broccoli in profusion. He palped the peppers gently, letting his thumb luxuriate in their clefts. He bought eggs, ground coffee, two bars of soap (there was a sale on), washing-powder, and proceeded up the stairs to his two-room apartment, now called 'studio'

8

even in this undistinguished quarter.

Having put the shopping-bag at his feet he unlocked the double lock. Break-ins were everyday. He had gone up the four flights breathing easily. Having put away his purchases and slipped out of his scarf and jacket, he tested. He opened the window and looked steadily in the direction of the dome of the basilica of the Blessed Martyrs. It rose westward, in a direct line across the morning-lit sea of roofs. Testing. He knew that the dolphin rampant on the ancient weather-vane wore a coronet with four fleurons. He noted three. Then five. He covered one eye with his hand which smelled faintly of cheese. Then the other. He stood for a spell. Then lowered the blinds, drew the curtains against the spreading light, undressed, and set the alarm for three in the afternoon. There was, he remembered, a meeting.

[3]

Meetings. How many had he attended in a lifetime? Even his martinet memory could not marshal the lot.

The first, to be sure, remained unforgettable. It took place during the bestial civil war between the Fascist legionnaires, still nesting in their barracks and scouring the blacked-out streets for the partisans, democrats, deserters, fugitives. It had been a clandestine meeting, in the boiler-room of the municipal baths, the building itself having been almost flattened by liberating bombs. He remembered the prickling odour of chlorine and burnt plaster, his father's hacking cough amid the muted voices, and going to bed hungry. His very first political meeting, and his father's defiant pride as they stole home by circuitous alleys and waste ground to the accompaniment of scattered gunfire out of the thick dark.

Meetings innumerable during his time of probation as messenger and sweeper on the shop-floor: syndical organization, wage protests, strikes, meetings to hear shop stewards and more elevated union officials. There stayed with him the brusque silence of the presses and the drone of oratory by city voices raw with tobacco and lack of sleep. Some time thereafter (he knew the date and hour), baptism: when Tullio took him along to hear a lecture on surplusvalue in Marxist and Leninist theory. It was delivered by a sweating doctoral student, behind thick glasses whose reflections darted oddly around the brown and green stucco in the packed room. His very first Party meeting. *In memoria*, inviolate, as was also, in that same wild month – the bells had been proclaiming freedom and chewing-gum – his first serious experience of sex. More meetings and yet more before he was admitted into that freemasonry of hope. The handshake all around, the austere fever of enlistment, the Party card thrust, with affected calm, into the pocket of his overalls and Tullio's joy at brotherhood within brotherhood.

After that, meetings were legion. Lessons on Marxist social theory, on the heritage of Gramsci, industrialization, the tactics of proletarian protest, the place of women, of the media, of sport, of the arts and sciences, primary and secondary education in a classless state. Films on life in the Soviet Union and analyses of its vanguard destiny. Meetings, obligatory, on Party funding, on the recruitment of new members, on electoral propaganda and discipline, on deviance and fractionalism. Sessions devoted to the composition and dissemination of tracts and posters (he was to be made secretary for information and publication). He could remember heated gatherings at the time of the great anti-imperialist, anti-Nato riots and general strikes. Meetings to gather money for comrades with cracked skulls, for the locked-out and the blacklisted. How well he could recall the commemoration, airless, opaquely vibrant as in a sealed chamber, of Stalin's death. They had become orphans huddled in sombre bewilderment. Tullio in tears. A few months later, there had been his only encounter with Palmiro Togliatti, when he had travelled, with other local delegates and committee members, to the rally and plenary assembly in beflagged, red-draped Bologna. He remembered the leader's sharp smile and the thunder of concordant voices. Meetings at the level of the cell, of the district, of the Party's regional executive so frequent and repetitive that he could no longer distinguish them.

Until the command performance, in the derelict cinema rented for signal occasions, during which he, so frugal of words – for only a written statement can be checked, made intractable to error and false memory – had spoken at length about the evident potential for a Fascist resurgence and CIA-financed coup from inside the Hungarian uprising, about the notorious Jew-hatreds of the Cardinal and his White Guard acolytes, about the tragic but unquestionable need (the phrase he actually used was 'dialectical logic') for Soviet intervention. Short of breath but pressing on. The imperialist and plutocratic powers were only waiting for just the tragic, yes, tragic misprision and macabre accident represented by events in Budapest. Witness their actions over the Suez canal. The motion of total solidarity must, therefore, be passed, the complete adherence of the local Party branch to Central Committee resolutions in Rome must be made manifest.

The pitch of his own voice during that long afternoon and evening stayed with him. As did Tullio's look of desolate love, of a man flayed alive at the moment when his exclusion, together with that of seven other revisionist

11

saboteurs and crypto-Trotskyites, was carried unanimously. Eerily he could hear, as from some archive of echoes within himself, the thud of the baize door as the seven men and the one woman, who was Maura, left the hall.

He had not attended his own ostracism, which came after Prague. Given his intervention during the session called to approve of the Soviet invasion, that ostracism was now as foregone as death itself. Had he not cited Lenin's suppressed testament which revealed the menace posed by Stalinist bureaucracy; had he not adverted to the penitential verities of the Twentieth Party Congress revelations of corruption and the cult of personality; had he not alluded, transparently though without naming him, to Trotsky's model of spontaneous and permanent revolution of the kind, he treacherously inferred, they had witnessed during the Prague Spring? Automatically, the next meeting would be his last. The summons had reached him. Together with the agenda on which his refusal of adequate self-criticism, his violation of Party democracy and discipline, figured amid matters arising.

During what he knew to be the relevant hour he had sat in his room, motionless, made stone. He had sat like a paralytic, his temples pounding as in a cold fever. Knowing that he was being read out of the scroll of the saved, of the elect to hope and meaning. The loneliness of that hour branded him irreparably. It was more solitary than death. He dragged himself to the staircase, intent on going to work, but found himself incapable of useful motion. His legs shook and the nausea made the stair-well spin. He took sick-leave and immured himself in his leprosy. Till Tullio hammered at his door, insistent.

The Circle for Marxist Revolutionary Theory and Praxis numbered less than twenty active members, but met almost as regularly as the Party sections.

And now, as he entered, the props and smells in the school-room (made available at nominal cost by the grace of one of the faithful, a primary school-teacher), were not much different from those which he had known during his long stay in the belly of the whale.

[4]

'Tullio.'

'*Professore*.'

The old, heart-warming joke. Consecrating with that fictive title one whose schooling had been rudimentary but whose physique, with its gaunt concavities, was indeed a touch professorial. More emphatically, that greeting did label a man whose obsessive scruple in respect of the minutiae of print, whose bristling distaste in the face of the approximate and the loosely mistaken, were magisterial and pedantic to a degree.

They shook hands with that hint of mock ceremony which intimate friendship fosters. Handshakes all around, in an aura reassuringly familiar and low-key. Chalk-powder, the odours of scuffed linoleum, the light-bulb slightly fugged under its ripped shade. Why, he wondered, were the light-bulbs at all such meetings inevitably both grimed with dirt and aggressive, dispensing a yellow, sick-room sheen? Why were the flowers on the desk or podium, even when exalted characters from the regional or national roster came to speak, so waxen? Idle thoughts, when he wanted to concentrate on Anna B.'s report. Comrade Anna. Why his notice of the down, slightly moist, on her upper lip, that hint of a moustache to come?

He tautened and focused on what she was saying.

But the word 'laundromat' kept recurring in so desultory a manner as to make his attention veer. Anna was seeking to analyse the lacunae in classical Marxist social theory revealed by the 'horizontal solidarities' which had developed and coalesced 'spontaneously' – a perilous, crucial adverb – in the working-class high-rise apartment buildings and estates at the new rim of the city. In these solidarities, in the crèches and launderettes inherited lines of class loyalty and militant activism (Anna's tone was momentarily vibrant) traditional demarcations, such as that, for example, between clerk and heavy-goods transporter, were being blurred or frankly eroded.

The dartings to and fro across natural divides of class interest and ideology were, in the main – and Comrade Anna paused slightly – the result of women's clusters. It was the unplanned conviviality of women around the laundromat and the coffee dispenser which wove new alliances and political-social impulses.

The speaker glanced up from her notes. Had anyone, she challenged almost reproachfully, bothered to investigate the radical differences in social infrastructure and peer-group communication as between coffee drawn from, and consumed near, a mechanical dispenser and that brewed in one's own kitchen and poured into one's own cups for a neighbour specifically welcomed and hosted? The new impulses, she reported, were of an essentially consumer-oriented category. This was natural enough and, in its own way, to be welcomed. But the inherent contradictions, the dialectically negative feedback, needed to be understood and fought against. The class struggle in which husbands were inevitably engaged, the combat for better wages, shorter hours and improved safety in the factory were of a kind with which the women, the wives and mothers, found it increasingly difficult to identify. A significant portion of the men and indeed of the women living in the industrial estates were now white-collar, though, to be sure, the percentage among women remained small. These transitional phenomena were, as yet, ill understood. (Too often in his hearing, in his participation in discussions across the long years, had 'ill-understood' been the saving phrase, that which made the suspect or tenebrous visage of the future bearable and the frank insight worth shelving.)

Anna B. went on. There were checkers, counter-personnel, assistant managers at the trucking depot who acted, exactly as Marxist analysis postulated, as parasites on exploited labour. But as their wives mingled with those of the true proletariat on terms of easy intimacy and 'collusive desires' – Anna let this phrase echo, as if in troubled evocation of her own privileged employment as a statistician in the psychiatric social service of the General Clinic – as their daily contacts grew more cohesive, the very concept of the political tended to fade away. What had Marxist and Gramscian sociology to contribute to a better understanding of these 'gender-bonded and gender-oriented socializations'? Had Kautsky or C. Wright Mills said anything to the point?

A certain gloom hung over the Comrade's closing queries. A gloom thickened by the acknowledgement that her untiring efforts to attract even a single potential recruit from the teeming warrens east of the river to the Circle's discussion-evenings had failed. Not a single one. He had managed to listen closely. But had he, at a point of especial gravity, caught the imp in Maura's eyes? Was it her bench, that worn school-bench incised to the grain with initials, sobriquets, minor obscenities and arrowed hearts, which had creaked in such irreverent accompaniment to Comrade

Anna's report? 'It is necessary to dream' (Lenin, 1902). But not, he reminded himself severely, to day-dream. And at that very moment, Anna having been duly thanked and her most valuable paper having been earmarked for detailed discussion at a later occasion, the members present, ten or eleven in all, turned to him, to the *Professore*, for what had come to be known, in affectionate irony, as the 'homily'. At successive meetings, it was he who glossed the news of the preceding two or three weeks, as culled from *their* newspapers and from *ours* – though no actual newspaper or even review, save a cyclostyled and infrequently distributed bulletin, genuinely reflected the views of the Circle. His commentary drew on eminent foreign papers as well, which his schooled eye sped across in the reading-room of the public library in his *quartiere*, that of Saint Jerome in the Marsh.

What could, what should he say tonight? What must he say if he was to deserve the trust of those now turning towards him (by instinct he always took a seat at the rear)? If Tullio and Maura were to continue being his? He caught himself staring at the wall-map of the nation, as displayed in every school-room. He was trying to isolate, among its four colours and infinitely familiar contours, the location of the escarped valley in Sardinia from which came his preferred cheese, the one he had bought and eaten that very day. The island shape was plain enough, as was its capital city in heavy type. But the detail, the recess in which that valley shone, swam before his eyes.

[5]

News from Prague and the German Democratic Republic, he observed, clearing his throat and bending forward slightly, was indeed difficult to interpret. The facts looked to be undeniable, though dramatized and cheapened by the western media. Thousands were storming embassies, camping at rail-heads and streaming towards the borders. Surface motives were plain enough. The socialist and Marxist regimes had been overtaken by ferocious exasperation, by a breakdown of elementary trust between government and governed. It was worth recalling (he felt the sadness in his bones as he said it) that Gramsci had warned of just such a contingency, of the corrosive fatality of 'family quarrels' in the wake of the Milan and Bologna strikes in the 1920s. But it was the task of the Circle to probe deeper, to lay bare the true nerve of history. The phrase was pompous; he knew it as he heard it out of his own mouth. Could it be that, once again, and in grim similitude to what historians told of the Dark Ages, migrations were thrusting westward out of a deprived, turbulent and inchoate east?

'What about the cars?'

Cesare Lombardi's interruption arrested his train of thought.

'Cars?'

'They are abandoning their cars. Thousands of them. They are dumping them at the frontiers or giving them away. I've seen it on television. Men and women kicking their cars and leaving them in the ditch.'

Friend Lombardi did have a gift for angular queries. He launched his circuitous darts from a stooped posture, eyes downcast, perspiring behind his tortoise-shell glasses.

'I know that.' (Patiently.)

Lombardi breathed heavily. He chain-smoked, as if the hunger which he had traversed during the last years of the war, when he crawled from lair to lair in fear of denunciation as a half-Jew and known anarchist, had never left him.

'Their cars are miserable. It is said you can smell their exhaust for miles. But imagine abandoning them. Just like that!'

He warmed to his theme, gathering it in like a faintly repulsive quarry.

'I ask you: why do they have all those foul machines in the first place? Polluting, wasting raw materials, consuming fossil fuels. It's pure lunacy. As bad as capitalism. Worse. When we know that bicycles will do for ninety per cent of our actual daily needs. That bicycles are clean and silent. And that a proper public transport system can provide for the rest. Those herds of stinking cars by the roadside. Don't you see what that really means? It makes no difference whether we live over here or over there. Even the worst of those automobiles' (the epithet which Lombardi appended was an old-fashioned, eroded obscenity) 'is totally beyond the reach of the Third World. Imagine what a doctor in Angola or Peru or China would give for even one of those Trabants. For the energy they consume, a useless dream, I know' (the point of his cigarette drew an angry arc) 'but one which hundreds of millions of human beings in Africa, Asia and Latin America would pay for. Every bloody and killing day of their wretched existence. Can you imagine what these men and women feel when they see those pictures of junked, abandoned cars and homes and jobs? There can be no life worth living on this pillaged earth, no justice worth having so long as . . .'

Lombardi paused to draw breath.

'Your analyses make me ill. Don't you see? We must learn to make do. Each and every one of us. With essentials. Using our legs to walk or pedal. Baking one decent sort of bread and not ten cellophane kinds. Our forests are going to pulp because there are a hundred – or is it more? – girlie magazines on the kiosks. We fly half-empty jumbos to cities already served by a dozen other airlines. Now cars are being littered by the side of the road like used Kleenex. To each according to his needs. Blessed Karl Marx! Does no one remember what real needs are? How few. How richly they could be satisfied? Superfluity enslaves. We have gone mad with superfluity. In the shanty-towns of Rio or Soweto – have you seen those television pictures? – families try to stay alive under bits of corrugated tin and rubber, next to open cess-pits. Every one of those tossed away Trabants could shelter . . .'

His incensed delivery failed him. Being corpulent, addicted to nicotine, a tireless collector of vintage jazz records and memorabilia, Cesare Lombardi, telephone engineer by profession, harboured a burning predilection for images of asceticism, for ideals of saintly privation. He dreamt of the Desert Fathers, of the Stylites, naked to the winds on their pillars of denial.

Father Carlo Tessone, sitting at an angle to him, knew this. Father Carlo, their only comrade from the Church, though his status had been, for some time, marginal. He, evidently, was a man who did not find it difficult to make do, to stay thin, to walk the city in his one patched garb and mended, high-laced boots. A self-denier with amused eyes and a touch of courtliness in his spare gestures.

Now Father Carlo spoke softly.

'Lombardi, to hear you one might think that Marxism must arrive at deprivation. That a just, proletarian distribution of resources and of the means of production is, after all, a sort of monasticism in the barrens. A clerisy of abstinence.'

Father Carlo let this elegant phrase fall with a hint of embarrassment. He had, he knew, a weakness for eloquence. No abnegation there but the old schooling at the seminary in rotundity and rhetoric.

The *Professore* realized he must take the reins.

'Yes. This is one of the charges brought against us. Against all Marxist models. That ours are the politics and institutions of backwardness. I remind those present here of the debates on this very issue in Plekhanov and Veblen. Is Marxism at bottom a strategy for survival in underdeveloped or stagnant economies, is it inherently alien to material progress and consumer-oriented social structures? When it is, so manifestly, a product, an analytic science, a discovery of historical laws, sprung of the industrial revolution and of the expansion of planetary resources?'

Tullio interjected. His tone was oddly neutral, which made his question the more ominous.

'*Professore*: those East German Trabants. Why should they be so undesirable? Why can a Marxist economy, in a country with a history of industrial strength and a skilled work-force, not produce a satisfactory internal combustion engine and chassis? Isn't that the real question?'

Further voices chimed in. The discussion eddied. It was inconclusive and, at times, ill-tempered.

He had to get to work. Outside the unwashed windows, the bells had sounded vespers. It was agreed that the questions raised would be further argued as events unfolded in the east. Leaving – renewed handshakes and the shuffling on of raincoats – he noted Maura's nod. It was, he judged, imperceptible to anyone else. It signalled Sunday.

[6]

Weather permitting, they met at the end-station of the tram-line in Via Alba. Then took the rackety train which looped the hill towns and villages to the north of the city. Maura brought the sandwiches and the fruit. The coffee thermos and bottle of wine were his responsibility. Sometimes he felt lavish and added cheese or a jar of olives. Without any particular destination in mind, they would alight at one or another of the small stations, punch the gravel with their walking-sticks and head upward. In the past, Tullio had quite often come along; once or twice Lombardi had puffed in their wake. Even Anna B. had been of the party, blushing at her hobnailed, sensible boots and tight trousers. But not of late. Maura and he had become, so distinctly, a couple.

The air was soft with October's end but had in it the uncertain light of the coming rains. Crossing the village, they passed the door, left ajar, of the church, and heard the muffled echoes of Mass. Soon the cracked voice of the single bell would chime briefly to the hills. They took the goat-track which meandered skyward through the laurel, the thorn-bushes and the fallow strips of stubble, scratched as if with bare hands and blackened nails out of the jumble of rocks.

The valley fell away quickly. Turning back he and Maura could see, even of a Sunday, the dun scarf of pollution unwound across the city and the new industrial zones. But here, above the dozen rust-tinted roofs and Verzani (they had noted the name on the station-master's hut), the folds of air shook softly as the last of the summer winds sang past, bound southward, he fancied, to nest and noise in the broken barns, in the almost spectral, bleached hamlets from which migrant labour was now pressing north. And as in

21

rebound to his thought, a train-whistle shrilled in the valley, on the main line, with its second-class carriages ferrying the uprooted and the bewildered to the slums of the cities.

He drew a long breath, saw Maura's lithe back rounding a turn in the trail just above him, and inhaled a faint trace of thyme. Soon now the sun would top the ridge and Maura would pause to strip off her jumper, knotting it around her hips under the rucksack. Her motion made his heart loud.

It was she, roughly ten yards ahead of him, who shading her smoke-grey eyes, pointed to a hollow in the overhanging screed. The very recent first autumn rains and gusts of colder wind had splayed the bushes. Something whitish and shaped shone in the little dell. They cut to the left through barbed grass. His metal-tipped cane struck a fallen, flat piece of stone paving. The impact rang bright. Other stone fragments lay near under the overhang of rock and tufa. Barely visible in the tangle of heather and striated chalk stood a small column, its fluting encrusted with lichen. Maura gave a low, cheery cry. The carved stone was cracked and at an angle, but her fingers could trace remnants of lettering. They knelt side by side. The air was still and warm in that hollow place. Minutely, he began brushing the mud and the lighter shards of rubble and crystallized rock from the graven lines. Maura turned to him inquiringly. He caught the nearness of her cheek and the embers in her hair. She was not, he supposed, beautiful. Only so much more than that.

They had, he proposed, chanced on one of the numerous miniature shrines or modest family memorials which dotted these hills. He added, with a pedantry which at once amused and embarrassed him, that these dated from the palaeo-Christian period, at the ebb-tide of the decomposing Roman empire, when Christendom flourished in the silent places. This site must, he ruled, be marked on the fifty-metre scale archaeological survey in the *Museo municipale*.

Now he extracted the large old-style handkerchief from his pocket (Maura always smiled at the gesture) and began cleaning the incisions. He blew neatly at the detritus and cleared the thin branches that had made their bed of the antique marble. Maura's shoulder warmed his arched back.

The text was fractured and eroded nearly beyond supposition. It ran between shallow double-borders and a motif, perfunctorily carved, which might, he guessed, be acanthus leaf. In one of the whorls a snail had left its indelible mark. Hurried labour, he reflected, the work of unskilled or hunted hands using, almost certainly, an earlier pagan site and votive stone for their urgent purpose.

'How can you be so sure that this is a Christian marker or inscription?'

Instinct. He might be wrong. But his fingers read the chiselling, the style of the letters as fourth-century, late third at the earliest. And although he could not be confident of making out correctly the roughened, largely effaced emblem, he could swear it was that of a fish, crudely drawn, between two stars. The symbol of the Son of God, the contours of resurrection so common in early Christian lapidaries and cult objects.

'*M*,' said Maura.

'And *N*. I can't make out the letter in between.'

His fingers passed and repassed delicately over the lost braille.

'*E* and *T*.' He spelt out the two letters with assurance.

'*MANET*.' And in this buried spot, the sun now full above them, his voice boomed. For he was certain of his reading.

The words, following only edges and the remembrance of scoured angles and curves which worked stone retains across time, could only be guessed at. But he had little doubt. The rotundity of the *O* was live to his thumb. No hand or eye acquainted with the serration characteristic of the stem of the capital *R* in the early Christian or late Roman stone-carver's alphabet could mistake the word or, more precisely, its certain shadow.

'*AMOR*.' He spoke the four letters with gentle triumph.

'*MANET AMOR*.' Love remains. Love endures.

'You are making it up,' whispered Maura, but repeated the Latin.

'The name must have been on the upper half of the tablet. A child's name, I think. Given the size of the stone. A child gone. Here, in these hills. When the family was under way, perhaps. Fleeing, or just crossing the col to join another community. A Lavinia, a Drusilla, of whom love remains.'

'It could just as well have been a little boy,' objected Maura.

He nodded, and his heart drummed.

She asked: 'Ought we to have uncovered it?'

'The rains did that. And the winds.'

'They did not read the words. If we found a letter fallen on the road, would we read it?'

'This letter, Maura, was meant for us.'

He felt awkward at the sound of his own intensity, hearing in that banality the hunger. But she nodded lightly and smiled. They rose to their feet. She peeled off her sweater and looked about for a moment. They propped their sacks and sticks against the warming stone. Again, he tasted a touch of thyme in the air and the secret scent of lavender late in the parting year. He half-closed his eyes so as to take in fully the brush of her clothes as she slipped out of her jersey and hiking pants. She glided her arms

24

behind her back and he could hear the hooks open. The ground was strange under his feet. When he stretched beside her, she was naked.

[7]

He had given television a wide berth. After the night's proof-reading it was sensible to allow his eyes all possible rest. The afternoon programmes, which he could have switched on, were, he knew, trash: housewives' striptease, family quiz shows and morose comedians out of the hinterland. Maura's insistence that they should install themselves in front of the little screen on that late November Sunday evening had irritated and disturbed him. Now he sat mesmerized.

Father Carlo had joined them. There was no television in the broom-closet of a room which he occupied fitfully at the hostel. He had brought a bag of macaroons of which the *Professore* was inordinately fond. The grit of almonds and burnt sugar clung happily to one's teeth. The padre too was spellbound, hunched forward on the kitchen stool, so compact in his observance of the screen that his weight and occasional shuffle seemed shadowy.

The titles, credits and presenter's overture had been breathless. Pictures, action sequences, interviews, exclusive documentary footage would be shown over the next two hours to mark 'the greatest wave of revolution, the greatest blossoming of freedom history had ever known'. There would be expert commentaries from Minister X, Professor Y and novelist Z. They would, in turn, join a panel assembling further luminaries of the political spectrum and of sociology. As the celebrated compère spoke, his mouth an almost perfect o of bounteous excitement, bursts of Beethoven deployed their great wings on the sound-track, and the chorale of the Ninth rose towards the fiercely spotlit Brandenburg Gate.

First came the Berlin saga and the crumbling of the Wall. Once again, the screen showed a wave of humanity pouring through jagged rents, climbing over wire. Border guards grinned vacantly and reached for cigarettes as do the bears in a bankrupt circus. Shots of teenagers from the east tumbling into West Berlin supermarkets, rocking in wonder before the shelves, emptying them in a sleep-walker's sweep. Bright-tinted toothpaste, lacquer for toenails, soft toilet-paper in the hues of the rainbow, deodorants, tights finely meshed and stippled, jeans bleached or mended. Sunglasses for the night, amplifiers, cassettes, coffee-beans from Brazil being whipped off the shelves and display cases. The reporter's lens and microphone homed in on a bounding, guffawing troupe, their carrier-bags piled high with video cassettes and sun-bright plastic rainwear. One of the lads mouthed his message straight into the bobbing mike: 'Horror-films, man. Porno. Hot lips, man.' And the girls in his wake screeched with joy and did a twist on the pavement. The camera swung back to the Wall itself and to the idle bulk of the Gate. Politicians embraced. A film star (minor) signed autographs on the platform of a watchtower. At every instant, the throng grew larger and more torrential.

Cut, and over to 'our colleague in Prague'. The bells pealing across unkempt gables. Havel on the balcony. 'Freedom . . . nation . . . democracy.' Eyes misted, the whirlpools of sudden laughter and tears in the crowd, the voices echoing from group to group, from parade to parade, the multitude at once empowered and set free. Newsreel shots of Soviet tanks in 1968, on the exact same street-corners where the Czechs now stood in recollection and soft drunkenness as if the very wind, clanging with bells, were alcohol.

The ads rolled on. Then Warsaw and Gdansk. A gross memorial to the Soviet liberators of 1944–45 being toppled into a cloud of brown dust. Brief collages of the death-ditches at Katyn, of Stalinist edifices against a sullen sky. Then the early images of Solidarity, of that walrus-man with the obstinate eyes and slow triumphs. An interview with a foreman outside a steel-mill: 'We have nothing left. We must begin again at zero. They stole everything. Communist bandits. Filth.' Close-up of his bony face, of hands sand-papered like those of the unfed in some African drought.

The first of the pundits, in a professorial study. Yes. He agreed entirely. 'An earthquake. Promethean. The liberation of the human spirit from the shackles of Marxist–Leninist folly and despotism. May I emphasize "Leninist"? You will be so good as to recall, *cara* Valeria' (the interviewer nodded supportively) 'the book in which I pointed out, many years ago, oh, the clairvoyance and confidence of one's youth, that so-called "Stalinism" is nothing more than an ineluc-table development, I stress "ineluctable", my dear friends, of the homicidal Leninist, indeed Marxist, blueprint.' At which pronouncement, the camera glided tastefully behind the sage's brow to show a panorama of the Milan skyline.

Now back to the action. To a meeting of the Hungarian Democratic Centre. Demands for the immediate withdrawal of Soviet forces. Immediate. Pictures of the walled-in bar-racks on the outskirts of Budapest, of women and children shaking their fists at Red Army sentries, teenagers with glazed faces and cheap plastic gun-belts. A capsule-chat with the new Minister of the Interior. 'We do have the infrastructure here in Budapest. Remember our illustrious economists. But help is needed. Urgently. Investment, *Signore*, and more investment. As I told my friend Andreotti, democracy costs money. In this whole building there is hardly a phone left that works. Not a single fax-machine at my disposal!' Arms outflung in quixotic despair and resolution.

'We are taking you to Sofia. Exclusive.' The presenter's vibrato rose. 'Pictures not seen before. A people on the march.' Fields. A file of men, women and children in embroidered blouses following a flower-decked tractor. A village hall. Editorial apologies for the quality of the sound. A large man, his braces sweated through, yelling into a small loud-hailer. Something about the price of oats and those Bolshevik locusts in Sofia. The assembly in response: 'Down with the Communists. Zhivkov to the lantern.'

A second break for ads. Motor-scooters circling a house-high Jeroboam of alcohol-free champagne. 'Safety bubbles,' crooned the young woman, her adam's apple pulsing ecstatically.

The round table, which was to crown the programme, had harvested politicians, more professors, the winner of this season's stellar prize for fiction (was the man lightly rouged?).

'Oh, there could be no doubt. No shadow of a doubt. History had turned on its hinges. The nightmare of state socialism was lifting. It was plain as daylight: Marxism had led to the Gulag and the massacres at Timisoara. To the extermination and enslavement of millions. To those cunning falsehoods which had suborned and infected western sensibility.' ('Sensibility' dropped subtly from the novelist's pursed lips and was taken up in caressing counterpoint by the eminent psychologist.)

28

Communism? *Finis.* Only Cuba, Yemen and Albania – but Albania for how much longer? – left in red on the world map. 'An unholy trinity, dear colleagues and treasured spectators.' Decorous mirth around the tinkling water-bottles. The evident problem was Russia itself. How long before it broke into pieces, its deprived millions trudging westward? How long before the Baltic republics, the vast Ukraine, Armenia, Georgia, Uzbekistan, little Moldavia, Siberia itself (who could foretell?) declared their independence from the impotent centre?

The bald historian urged caution: 'These seismic movements take time. Russian patriotism . . . the hydrogen bomb and space programme. After all . . .'

But the syndicated columnist tugged impatiently at his bow-tie and offered wagers to all participants: 'The USSR will collapse within eighteen months. There will be anarchy when the soldiers come home. Pogroms. Bread riots. Yeltsin is ready to make his move. I have it on highest authority. From the horse's mouth, believe me! Within a year and a half. Perhaps less. *Kaput.*' And he passed his hand across his wind-pipe, the heavy signet ring glinting.

The moderator turned brusquely to Comrade Gabrieli of the Central Committee in Rome. 'Well, *Dottore*?'

A final bouquet of ads. To maintain suspense. To prepare the audience for revelation.

Why was Gabrieli ill-shaven? The idiotic thought pressed on Maura.

'We are, as you know, committed to a multi-party democracy. We have been for a long time. Even Togliatti . . . This present crisis . . . how shall I put it?'

He lunged at the television and stabbed at the switch. Neither Father Carlo nor Maura moved. The sofa, the book-shelves, the stool brought in from the kitchen, lay in darkness. He glanced at the plants in the window-box. Their leaves hung motionless. Rubbery. Maura turned on the table-lamp (it had been his first gift to her) and brought coffee. Father Carlo stretched and massaged his thin back.

Leaving, the *Professore* almost tripped over the door-sill. Maura caught his elbow: 'You must see the eye-doctor. You *must*.'

She had urged it under her breath, but Carlo, who had preceded him down the murky stairs, turned and looked back.

[8]

'Not for this!'

He heard himself repeating the phrase. The pink and yellow flashes from the window display of the all-night video-rental shop made his cheeks clown-like and his eyes blink.

Father Carlo grinned at him.

'Careful, *Professore*. That's been *our* line. Not for *this* world. Not for the filth and lucre and beatings of this life. There must be something better. Since that day when they drove the nails into his hands and feet. There just had to be something beyond bread and circuses.'

Father Carlo's cadence seemed to mime and tease his own.

'It would be unbearable if it had all been only for this. As you say, old friend. All that pain, the dirt up to our eyeballs. If this turned out to be the be all and end all, the sum total, we would do best to hang ourselves on the next lamp-post. On the next meat hook. When the great white dawn didn't come and set Galilee or Samaria alight, there were those

30

who did hang themselves or pitch themselves head first into wells. They had seen the black sun on his dead eyes, on his torn flesh. All for nothing. So they did away with themselves. Many did it again when the year one thousand came and went, with the usual rain and the customary plagues and the ordinary famines. And they'll do it again, on the first common morning of the year two thousand. Shouting: "Not for this! It's been too long. How can it all have been only for this? The promise and the desolation."'

Father Carlo continued:

'That's where we came in. The Mother Church. With the aspirin. Gently now, good children. Don't swallow too fast. Let it melt in your mouths. Wrap it in a wafer. Wash it down with a sip of wine. Gently. For it is his body and watery blood. Spilt for you, and now within you. The pain-killer. So that you can endure. Till Sunday week. In your garbage lives, in your hunger and lice, in the incontinence of the geriatric ward or that of the new-born cretins. Just another little week to crawl through. Till the next medication. Let the promise fill your empty bellies. His kingdom will come. Not quite yet, not here in any real sense, but without fail: in the tomorrow after tomorrow's tomorrow.

'Observe our mercies. Do not rage at injustice, at the wealth flung in your face, at the torture of the innocent and the helpless. Do not lament your own misery. Do not flash your broken teeth against your children's hunger. These are but passing trials. Bear them meekly. Give the slaughter-house men a smile, bow to the rich, cast down your eyes when the depraved roar past. Theirs may be the rewards here and now. Yours are yet to come. Acknowledge the cunning of my text. Order and obeisance in this vale of sorrows, compensation over there. Around the next corner of time.'

31

He had listened, his chin against the raised collar of his coat: 'Do you know what socialism is, reverend Father? Do you know what it really is?'

Father Carlo turned to him lightly: 'What is it, my friend? What is it really?'

'It is impatience. Impatience. That's what socialism is. A rage for now.'

And the spurt in his voice made him sound hoarse.

Father Carlo nodded: 'So it was in early Christianity. Exactly so. Impatience ran wild in Jesus. When he cursed the pitiful fig-tree, or when he said that he had come bearing a sword. When he bade the dead bury their dead or when he rushed into Jerusalem unprepared and ran riot in the Temple yard. His impatience may well have been more terrible than that suffered by any other living being. He was so impatient to enter into the mystery of his own beginning and become what he was. And what did Christ leave his little mafia? A treasure of impatience. They panted for the end of time like dogs dying of thirst. For the last sunset. They believed it to be imminent, a week away, a month at most. They smelled the huge rank smell of the end. They thought they saw the seals breaking on the book of life. But it didn't come to pass, did it? Or it came and went like snow at midnight, unnoticed. History had not pulled down the shutters. And we were back on the treadmill. Whereupon the Church ordered patience and more patience, and handed out tranquillizers.'

He laughed almost joyously: 'But you see there have been quite a few among us who never learned the arts of waiting. Heresy also is impatience. The heretic takes short cuts. We too have had our dreamers of tomorrow. Justice for everyman, as Jesus wanted. Peace upon earth. No more swollen bellies and to each according to his dignity and aspirations.

Tomorrow at daybreak. Or, at the very latest. Monday next.

'How effectively the Church has dealt with the impatient ones. The millenarians, the mendicants, the anabaptists, the Adamites, the Brethren of True Love, all the crazed preachers of a new Jerusalem! How it has scourged and erased them from history. Not a single text left of the Cathars, who taught perfection here and now. There is nothing Rome has dreaded more than impatience. His kingdom is not of this world. Has there ever been a more adroit political manifesto? Tell me, *Professore*.'

The two walkers found themselves looking at each other and so nearly in step.

'It is not only you socialists who have been impatient. Some of us have been pretty well mad with impatience, *mio caro*. For so long. But what earthly use has it been?'

Father Carlo stumbled over his own word. He took it up a second time with a chuckle.

'Earthly. That's the whole point, isn't it? Of what use has it been here *on earth*? How impatient Jesus must have been in that tomb. Three days can be a very long time. A small eternity. For us it's been longer.'

They had left the Corso. Unnoticing, they headed towards the river.

'Much longer.'

They crossed puddles of thicker blackness where the high, nailed-over portals of condemned palaces and tenements cast their night shadows.

Father Carlo was humming. A vacant, up–down tune. The hum of the Psalmist or of the half-woken monk in the chill of matins.

They caught the scent of the river. Tar and wisps of diesel.

*

'We did take that impatience from you. I know that, Carlo. But you were not the first. The hunger is much older. The rage was in Moses. The commandments of justice were his and the abstentions. Those endless inventories of what it is we must do without. Moses knew he couldn't enter the promised land. It would be too small for his fury.

'Have you read Amos, *reverendissime*? Only Communists now read the Bible. Amos was out of his mind with anger. At the greed which parades through the cities, at the empty eyes of the child beggars. All our impatience since seems to me like an echo of his voice. He knew. He knew the world in which grain is burned or rat-poisoned so that prices do not fall on the commodities exchange and in which children are sold on the night streets or set to labour in carpet factories and bead shops, fourteen hours at a stretch, till they go blind and tubercular. Amos had seen it all. He had heard the giggle of money and stepped in its vomit. And Jesus after him, I agree. "There shall come a time when men will exchange love for love, justice for justice." Not lucre for lucre. Was it an Evangelist? Was it Saint Francis or Mother Theresa? Tell me, Father Carlo, who prophesied thus? Marx did. Karl Marx. In 1844. When he was writing to and for himself. Putting impatience to paper. Not strategy or analysis or polemic. But prophecy and promise out of a great rage. The very beard of that man was angry.'

They had come on to the bridge.

Carlo's move: 'Moses and the Prophets. The man from Nazareth. Marx. Just as the Nazis said. Communism is Judaism writ large, the virus of Bolshevism is the Jew-virus.'

They were leaning over the wrought-iron balustrade, enamelled with pigeon droppings. His nails scraped idly at the stuff. Would Father Carlo, he wondered, perform the stock gesture out of morose French movies. Father Carlo

34

did. The match flared and arched from his fingers into the slow current below.

'I don't know much about Jews. I was young when it was done to them. But I have my own theory. That business about being a chosen people, the covenant with history. I believe in it. But not in the way they tell it, Father Carlo: it is the wretched who are chosen. It is those who are born into hunger, into AIDS. It is the congenitally deformed and the deaf-mutes. It is almost the whole cursed lot of us. The numberless tribe of the losers. God chose us to be those who wait. Till our waiting will grow so unendurable that justice and brotherhood must explode out of us. Have you ever looked closely at those waiting for the soup-kitchens to open, for the blankets they hand out in the doss house? They only *seem* like the dead. Look closer. Behind their eyes, a long dark way behind, the embers are alive. The thorn-bush is burning inside them. They are the chosen people of despair. But also of hope, Carlo.'

He had veered towards him, full-face: 'What the hell can a rich man hope for? Why bother with hope when your belly is full? That's what makes every victim a Jew, a real Jew. The truly chosen do not descend from Abraham, who was a millionaire. We do not come from Job, who doubled his holdings. We are the children of Hagar. We have fed on stones, and wasps have sung for us. There can be no Communist, no real socialist who is not, at bottom, a Jew.'

A string of barges, their lights reddish, passed underneath. The arches of the bridge resounded to the coughing motors.

As he stared at the receding lights, conviction quite overcame him: 'Do listen to me, Carlo. It sounds silly. But here is how I see it. When a man or woman is made an outcast, when they humiliate and spit at us, whoever we are,

35

wherever we may be, we become Jews. In that instant.'

'A dark syllogism, *Professore*. Look where it led.'

'But that's the whole point. Don't you see? The Jews refused to take the promissory note. To swallow what you call aspirin. They saw that nothing had changed after Jesus. Men ate men, just as before. Beggars remained beggars. So he could not be the Messiah, could he? Not the one worth waiting for, whose true coming would make a lit place of the world. Now and for ever.'

Father Carlo let a second match flare in his cupped hand and watched its descending glow, but said nothing.

'It does make sense, surely you see that? There were Jews who saw deeper and understood that the Messiah would never come. Never. Or rather, that the Messiah was man himself. That the revelation and the great winds to come were those of our own history. That ordinary men and women had not even begun to *be themselves*.'

He exulted at the obviousness of it.

'Men and women, creatures of reason, custodians of this earth: yes, there is a Messiah and a Jerusalem but not after one's funeral and not out of pink clouds. And there are laws, but not ones spewed out of some volcano in Sinai. There are laws of history, and science, and supply and demand. And if you need miracles, look around you! At the irrigation of a desert, at the finding of penicillin, at the invention of braille, at the ability of simple algebra to fix the exact location of a star a hundred million light years away. So many miracles that it's embarrassing. Why turn water into wine – any village conjuror can do that – when you can turn rags into paper and lead into print?'

He was talking too much. Orating. Pontificating as if in some third-rate allegoric novel. He flushed at the heat of his own voice. When he knew that talk came cheap, that his only true craft was that of silent print, which could be corrected, checked and checked again. Chattering away like one on the threshold of drunkenness.

They fell into step and crossed to the eastern quarters of the city. These had their own night hum. When Father Carlo turned to him they were on a flight of damp steps from the embankment to the tram-lines and to one of the tunnel-dark alleys which led from the river to Piazza San Severo.

'Miracles?'

Father Carlo had made the word sound sadder than any other in the language, and grimier.

'The miracles of reason and the laws of history? I don't know about you, *Professore*, but I can just about picture to myself, say, a thousand people. In a hall. Or, vaguely, a few thousand in a stadium. A figure like one million means nothing to me. I can't get any purchase on it. Twenty-five million. That we are told was the number of men, women and children Stalin starved, froze, tortured to death. Twenty-five. I can say the number but can grasp nothing of its reality, of its concrete meaning. So I focus on one single human being. On a nun they arrested for counter-revolutionary attitudes and sabotage some time in 1937. They transported her to Kolyma, to the Arctic Circle. In the hold that took prisoners from Vladivostok to the mines. On one of those hell barges, she begged and screamed for water. They pissed in her mouth, asked her whether it was as tasty as communion wine, and raped her. She was then told to make neat mounds of the earth and stones being hauled out of the shafts. The women had only a kind of raw shift to wear. In the summer many went mad, literally mad, with mosquito bites and swamp fever. Sister Evgenia lived into the winter. One day there was so little light on the tundra that she piled the stones without due care. They toppled over. She was beaten, on and off, for ten hours. Then she was sent back to pile them up again. No sleep allowed her. When she passed out, they poured ice water over her and made her stand to attention in the puddle. Her feet froze to the ground. Burning more horribly than in fire. Sister Evgenia stood there through the whole day. We have eye-witnesses. First she said out loud, "May God forgive you." Over and over. Then she crooned prayers and begged the Holy Mother to intercede for those who had beaten her. That evening the other women in the labour-squad had to chop down her body with an axe. Her eyes were still open.

'So I do my best to make Sister Evgenia stand for 24,999,999 other human beings done to hopeless death by your miracles! By your proud winds of history and scientific laws of social progress. I can't manage it. No brain can comprehend what your fine freedom did to man on this planet. There is not, just now, dear friend, a day when they are not digging up mass graves in the forests of the Ukraine, skulls by the ten thousands, each with a neat little bullet-hole in its back, skeletons, their wrists bound with wire so that the pain would grow worse till the moment of execution. That's what came of your Messiah for man. A savagery beyond understanding. Mass murder which makes the soul sick when one even tries to think of it. Arise ye prisoners of starvation. Oh yes: so that we can push you into the lime-pits. Break your chains. So we can flog you to death with them. Red dawn in the east. Light by which to kill and maim and reduce to cringing terror the millions of coolies from Beijing to Prague, from Kolyma to the Turkestan desert. As you say: they did irrigate those deserts. With blood. And there was penicillin: for the killers and court-jesters. Why, indeed, turn water into wine? A paltry trick, I agree.

When you can turn human blood and human sweat into gold and iron-ore.'

Father Carlo flung the question at him as out of some huge distance though they had kept the same pace. The narrow alley, with its rare, stove-in lamps hooked to the tenement walls, rang with their voices.

'Stalin was trained in a seminary. He was taught damnation and the blessed necessity of hell and had behind him a thousand years of anathema, of church despotism and censorship. Who has massacred more consistently than the churches?'

Carlo interrupted, flaring: 'For pity's sake. Not that old saw again. The Inquisition and Galileo. Even a novice dialectician could do better than that! Do you honestly believe that I don't know what suffering, what destruction the churches have caused? Do you imagine there is a day when I don't remember that Jew-hatred and the hounding of the so-called heretic sprang from the very first roots of Christianity, and feel sick to my soul? Can you believe that I would be with you tonight, *mio caro*, or be one of the faithful in our pitiful Marxist coven if I didn't know all that and worse?'

At the word 'coven' they both laughed loud and loosened. They had entered the trim square with its fountain. Undersized obelisks encircling nymphs and seahorses rotund and decrepit in their immemorial thirst. Odd, he reflected, how the ring and plash of a fountain is different at night-time. More subterranean, somehow. A chill blew from the plumes of water and he tightened his scarf.

'But there is a difference.'

The emeritus priest said it calmly: 'A cardinal difference, if you will allow the term. The crimes of the churches have been committed in the name of a revealed, transcendent verity. The fires were no less hot or the censorship less suffocating. I know that. On that level, there can be no apologia. But those who did these hideous things were labouring to save souls. They were betting on eternity. They held themselves, poor cruel imbeciles, to be God's agents. The stakes were so high, so pure and free of earthly benefit, that any sin would be a crime, an uncaring without end. But at the heart of Communism there is a demeaning of man and woman worse than the tyrannies and depravities in Christendom, foul as these are.'

Father Carlo stopped, fixed for an instant in his own perception: 'At the heart of Communism is the lie. The central, axiomatic lie: a kingdom of justice, a classless brotherhood, a release from servitude here and now. In this world. That's the great lie. The systematic bribing and betraying of human hope. The perversion is monstrous. To turn war into the word "peace", a continent of slave-labour into the motherland of socialist freedom. For seventy measureless years that perversion made human beings tremble in their rooms like trapped animals, re-wrote history according to the lunatic whims of the despot, rubbed out the names of the executed and the banished so that memory itself – memory, *professore* – would be emptied of truth, like a garbage-bin. So that the names could not be made a prayer. Sister Evgenia. Sister Evgenia of the frozen feet. Just speak it with me this once. She will hear us. She and the erased ghosts butchered not in the name of grace everlasting, but so that gangsters and hangmen and bureaucrats could fatten. Corruption without end. The lie in every nerve. What your scientific state-socialism produced was not even Satan's realm as the apocalyptics and the inquisitors foresaw it. It was something smaller, tawdrier, more inhuman. Like a world ruled by poisonous lice.

Your earthly messiahs turned out to be nothing but hypocritical hoodlums. Lords of lice.'

At the corner of the wider street was an all-night café, harshly lit. The steamed urns with their crowned tops and silvery sheen reminded Father Carlo of Torah scrolls he had seen in an exhibition of Jewish remnants. The thump of the juke-box could be heard even in the street, but as if muted by the dead hour. Its tired cadence blended with the beat of the fountain as it receded behind them. Sugary crumbs and rolls gone hard (the bakeries would open in about an hour) clung to the glass bells on the formica table-tops. But the coffee was hot and they cradled it in their hands. Father Carlo went back to the counter and bought two glasses of *Strega*. He set them down cautiously, brimful. From across the room, under the calendar of the *Mundial*, now sacred history, a woman flashed the two men a companionable leer. And fluttered her hands in some heraldic sign of complicity before slipping back and inward into the spongy deeps of her aloneness. Her hair must, he thought, have been at some point lustrous and even softer than Maura's.

'But now, Carlo? What now?'

'What then shall we do? A fine title. Lenin's most honest book. Written when he was powerless. An exile. What you would call "a Jew".'

'Consider the source of our error. Of that great lie. And mark you, I don't accept that it was. Or that there were only venal butchers at the top. Consider.'

Momentarily, he held the coffee in his mouth. It was good coffee, but as he swallowed and let the dusky heat seep through him, a greater tiredness seemed to follow.

'Marxism did man supreme honour. The Moses and Jesus and Marx vision of the just earth, of a neighbour's love, of

41

human universality, the abolition of barriers between lands, classes, races, the abolition of tribal hatreds: *that* vision was – we've agreed, haven't we? – a huge impatience. But it was more. It was an over-estimate of man. A possibly fatal, possibly deranged but none the less magnificent, jubilant over-estimate of man. The highest compliment ever paid him. The Church has held man in doleful contempt. He is a fallen creature, doomed to sweat out his life-sentence. Dust to dust. Marxism has taken him to be almost boundless in his capacities, limitless in his horizons, in the leaps of his spirit. A reacher to the stars. Not mired in original sin, but himself original. Our history is nothing but a savage prologue.

'A true Bolshevik, Carlo, owns nothing but the clothes on his back. No home. No family. No forgiveness if he breaches discipline or makes a mistake. Listen to me carefully: *he does not even have hope*. Not in your sense. No lilies and incense to come. No Mass said for his dead soul. He has something more unyielding than hope, more worthy of man's unmapped intellect and guts. The right words are hard to find. He has *insight*.'

He said it twice over.

'He understands his own condition and necessary suffering. He knows what defeat tastes like and even passing despair. There are 40,000 Communards, men, women, twelve-year-old boys, buried in mass graves under the shopping streets of Paris. The hopes of a Communist are a way of seeing with absolute clarity. Exactly as through a radio-telescope which brings us the facts about a universe infinitely older than the human race and which will evolve long after our extinction. Such seeing is clearer than hope. It honours man beyond every honour. That's where we went wrong.

'And never forget, *padre*, that there *have been* men and women, and more than just a handful, who lived up to the expectation of Marxism, who have *lived up*! Rosa Luxemburg when they clubbed her to death or the volunteers in the International Brigade or Gramsci, here, among us or the Communist partisans silent under torture. All deceived. But were they deceived? Who gave what medical aid they could in the starving villages, and kept faith in the Gulag, as your nun did, and died praising Stalin, knowing even in their own insane misery, that it was he who had made Russia capable of withstanding the Fascist onslaught. Mankind is not made up of saints and martyrs. It is not made up of those drunk with justice and possessed by reason. Yes, we got it wrong. Hideously wrong, as you say. But the big error, the over-estimate of man from which the mistake came, is the single most noble motion of the human spirit in our awful history. To me, to so many before me, it has compensated for our failings. It has made of that drunken slut over there something without limits. Every beggar is a prince of possibility.'

Father Carlo saluted the formula: 'You *are* a dialectician, old friend. Your health!'

The *Strega* went down like brown flame.

They took a second glass, and his hand shook a little as he brushed Carlo's sleeve.

'Capitalism never made this mistake. Don't you see? The free market takes man at his mean average. And *mean* is the word. It invests in his animal greed. It makes a balance sheet of his egotism and his petty interests. It caresses his appetites for goods and comforts and mechanical toys and holidays in the sun. Tickling his belly so that he rolls over and begs for more. Which keeps consumerism going.

Capitalism has not left man where it found him, it has lessened him. We are become a pack snarling for luxuries, grunting at the trough. That second car. A larger refrigerator. We are indeed possessed, more so than any of the crazed and the demonic in your manuals of witchcraft. By possessions possessed. By unnecessary, idiotic wants. To the pitch of mutual savagery and stupor. That's it Father Carlo, I have it now ... A kind of savage stupor or supineness. On the couch. In front of the television. Have you read about American children, aged five and less? Twenty-seven hours a week in front of the screen.'

He gestured towards the calendar on the café wall.

'A billion and a quarter viewers for the *Mundial*. What is your sacramental aspirin compared to television? Compared to the way in which men's dreams are packaged by advertisement. We make love according to the television images. We masturbate to the cadence of the video cassette. That is the very genius of capitalism: to package, to put a price-tag on men's dreams. Never to value us beyond our mediocrity. Ladies and gentlemen, the escalator awaits you. We are moving upward together. Towards better sun-tan lotions, towards a faster lawn-mower, to the deep-freeze of your wildest dreams and the stereo and white telephone next to your toilet seat. Hold on: the Holy Grail of cable-pornography for all is in sight. Look: there is the promised land, Disney-world for all. And there are gods, Carlo *mio*, in supermarket heaven. Madonna of the sequin tights. And Maradona, he of the hand of God. Has it ever struck you how those two names ...'

He broke off, emptying his drink at a draught. He should not have drunk that second glass. It thrust him forward. He was marooned in his own loquacity, the words thrashing about and spilling.

'The Cold War was no accident. No conspiracy concocted by power-brokers. Communism, perhaps even Stalinism, had horribly over-estimated man. As I said . . .'

He was repeating himself, he knew. Professorially. He couldn't stop: 'How accurately America has priced man, reducing him to well-being, making peace between human desires and fulfilment. Stalin starved millions. It's the truth. May he rot for it in hell everlasting. But America made the hungry, the drugged, the ugly invisible. Which is worse? It buttered the souls of men. No matter that the stuff is often margarine, oily, synthetic, golden-yellow. The colour of money. No matter. Fat-free, slim-line, daisy-sweet margarine on thirty kinds of bread. Carlo, I'm not making this up, they have thirty different sorts of bread over there: health-breads, croissants, seeded rolls, blueberry muffins, nut-breads, whole wheat, rye, pumpernickel, *panettone* for your dog, for your canary, all spread out in those California emporia.

'How stupid, how cruel it was of those nut-cases, of those prophets in their flea-bitten desert to make man homeless to himself. When there is Los Angeles.'

'Bullshit.'

Father Carlo said it without rancour.

'Bullshit, *Professore*. The old Party-line blood-libel on human nature and on America. About which, I mean American, you and I really know very little. To me it sounds like the society which says to every man and woman: "Be what you want to be. Be yourself. This world was not made only for geniuses or neurotics, for the obsessed or the inspired. It was made for you and you and you. If you choose to try and be an artist or a thinker or a pure scholar, that's fine. We will neither inhibit you nor put you on a pedestal. If you prefer

45

to be a couch-potato, an auto-mechanic, a break-dancer, a mile-runner, a broker, if you prefer to be a truck-driver or even a drifter, that's fine too. Perhaps even better. Because it so happens that ideological passion and ascetic illumination, that dogma and sacrifice, have not brought only light and aid to this approximate world of ours. They have sown interminable hatred and self-destruction." And when America says, "Just be yourself," it is not saying, "Do not better yourself." It is saying: "Go after that Nobel Prize if that's what fires your soul. Or that heated swimming-pool." Not because America believes that heated swimming-pools are the Parthenon or even a necessity. But because they do seem to bring pleasure, and not very much harm. "Move up the ladder, if you can," says America, "because the desire to live decently, to give your family a comfortable home, to send your children to schools better than those you attended yourself, to earn the regard of your neighbours, is not some capitalist vice, but a universal desire." Do you know, *Professore*, America is just about the first nation and society in human history to encourage common, fallible, frightened humanity to feel at home in its skin.'

'Not if that skin is black!'

'Even that is coming. Painfully, I know. But inevitably. American democracy . . .'

'In which, even at vital elections, only about thirty per cent exercise their right to vote . . .'

'But that's the point!'

Father Carlo was almost shouting: '"Vote if you will," says America. "Our education, our democratic system would have you vote. But if you are too lazy to bother, too ignorant, too bored, well, that's no catastrophe either. There's plenty of history ahead." It is under the Nazi boot, *Professore*, it is under the Stalinist truncheon that ninety-nine

46

per cent of all citizens cast their ballots. Do you prefer that to American waywardness?

'I do know this, my dear friend: there are in American affairs black pages, stupidities in plenty. But on balance, America does stand as the one and only great power and community which, unlike any other I know of, is aiming to leave the globe a little better off, a little more hopeful than it finds it. Hope has, in fact, been America's main gross national product and export. Think of Woodrow Wilson, of Roosevelt. Of Lincoln, above all. Ask, if you dare, the millions who have survived under Marxism–Leninism, whether they would rather endure such a regime a day longer, or be penniless immigrants to America or even tenants in an American slum. You know the answer. It is filling the air just now.'

'A country which no poem can shake. Where no philosophic argument matters . . .'

Carlo cut him off.

'I did once hear you declare, at one of those blessed meetings of the Circle, that to exile a man because he differs from you on Hegel and on points in Party orthodoxy is proudly to honour the human spirit. That stupid enormity still drums in my poor head. I have never heard a sane man expound anything more barbaric. If learning, if intellectual argument need to be honoured at that price, if they must feed on intolerance, on condescension, on fatuous authority, to hell with them!'

'Like you, *Professore*, I cannot abide Rock music. My stomach turns at most television, at the plastic and porn, fast food and illiteracy that pours out of what you call "California". But I wonder whether even these things are inflicting on men a fraction of the pain, of the despair which all our Athens, all our high culture have inflicted. They rocked

47

around the clock not long ago to raise millions for charity. They lectured on Kant and played Schubert and went off the same day to stuff millions into gas ovens.

'America may not be for you or me. Not for a Communist dreamer and glutton for the printed word. Not for a mendicant friar. But we two are museum exhibits. Incorrigible chatterers. We are ghosts out of the dark of history or pre-history, you said so yourself, *Professore*. Don't you understand? The tidal wave across the Berlin Wall and all the way to Prague and the Pacific is screaming with life. It is the insurrection of the young, even when they are eighty years old. Your dogma, your tyranny of the ideal, pumped youth out of human lives. Under despotism children are born old. Just look at their eyes and mouths in those pictures from Romania. And if America is childish, as it may be, what a lucky failing that is! Fountain of Youth? What he found may be Coca-Cola. But it does bubble!'

'It rots your teeth. You Jesuit. You casuistical Jesuit.'

They were walking again, briskly and aimlessly, towards the south-bound boulevard and the war memorial.

'We are, Carlo, a murderous, greedy, unclean species. But we have produced Plato and Schubert, to use your own examples, Shakespeare and Einstein. It follows that there are differences in worth between human endeavours. *Credo*: that it is intrinsically finer for a human being to be obsessed by an algebraic problem, a Mozart canon or a Cézanne composition than by the manufacture of automobiles or the trading of shares. That a teacher, a scholar, a thinker, even, God have mercy, a priest is almost immeasurably more valuable and nearer the dignity of hope than is a prize-fighter, a broker, a soap-powder magnate. *Credo* again: that the mystery of creative and analytic genius is just that, a mystery, and that it is given to the very few. But that lesser

48

beings can be woken to its presence and exposed to its demands. Oh I know, on a free vote it is the bingo-hall and the dog-track that will prevail, not the theatre of Aeschylus. I know that hundreds of millions of our fellow men prefer football to chamber music and would rather become glazed in front of a soap opera or blue movie than pick up a book, let alone a serious book. Amen to all that, says capitalism. Let their choice be free. Let them stew in their well-being. Hippos are free to wallow in their mud. Why not man? But that, Carlo . . .'

And once more they stood on the pavement facing each other.

'is to hold man in utter contempt. It is to turn history into a graveyard for used cars. Marxism tried otherwise. It filled the symphony halls and the libraries. It gave teachers and writers a living wage. What matters more, it gave them an eminent status in society; it made museums free of charge, open to all. It taught that a great theorem or sonata or philosophic principle comes nearer the bone of man, of our nascent humanity, than does the latest hit on a pop chart.'

The sounds in the air, even their own resumed motion, appeared to get busier with the imminence of daybreak.

'I agree with you, *Professore*. I wouldn't be feeling the wet pavement through my shoes if I didn't. I agree with every word, my dear orator. But I cannot see by what authority, by what right, you or I can cram *our* values – yes, they are mine too – down other men's throats. You claim to be arguing from love for the common man, from what you call an over-estimate of his means. But that love is filled with con-tempt and oppression. The pursuit of quality, your blueprint for excellence, comes with the lash. The price is too high. We have seen that.'

'Hypocrisy, Father Carlo, hypocrisy and cant! If you

49

honestly believed that, how could you be a priest, even half of one? How could you be a teacher, imparting knowledge to others, forcing it, as you put it, down their often unwilling throats? Every little step forward is made of sweat and mutiny. Until the insight is won, until the craft is mastered. No one has ever learned or achieved anything worth having without being stretched beyond themselves, till their bones crack. "Easy does it," says America to mankind. But easy has never done it. Never. I don't want to know how long it takes to produce a bottle of Coca-Cola or an instant hamburger or a tranquillizer. I do know that it takes six hundred years for the grapes to become what they are in those hills around us, six hundred years of back-breaking toil and silent cunning. Years in which hail almost flattens them or in which the heat is too fierce or during which they have been ploughed under.'

'Why, then, did you define socialism as impatience?'

'I don't know.'

As if at the edge of the pavement, in a stillness.

'Of late, I do get things muddled, Carlo. A slow impatience. Something like that.'

And abruptly, he seized his companion's elbow: 'I am a socialist. I am and remain a Marxist. Because otherwise I could not be a proof-reader!'

The self-evidence of it burst on him. He wanted to fling his arms wide, to dance on that very spot.

'If California triumphs, there will be no need of proof-readers. Machines will do it better. Or all texts will be audiovisual, with self-correctors built in. Night after night after night, Carlo, I work till my brain aches. So as to get it absolutely right. So as to correct the minutest misprint in a text which no one may ever read or which will be shredded the next day. Getting it right. The holiness of it. The

50

self-respect. *Gran Dio*, Carlo, you must see what I'm driving at. Utopia simply means *getting it right*! Communism means taking the errata out of history. Out of man. Reading proofs.'

He was out of breath. What a queer picture they must make, Carlo pacing, he on his toes, under the first distant volley of bells. Matins and the wail of a siren from the river.

'I can't match all your clever arguments, *mio* Carlo. You may even be right about America. And I know what they would have done to an outsider like myself – am I some sort of Leninist Albigensian? – over there, in the east. But I believe in my belief. What else is there for me now?'

More bells, out of unison, querulous and booming. An early bus drove past, and he saw the tow-headed driver yawning hugely. A metal shutter was cranked up, and electric light from a kiosk spilled down the road. Sunday morning sounds thickened at every moment. A bus in the opposite direction, just out of the depot.

Carlo said: 'Look at that sky-light over there. Under the chimney-pots. Just over there. Morning.'

He followed the pointing finger. To see better, he closed one eye.

[9]

'Open both eyes, if you please. Wide. Hold steady.'

The ophthalmologist's buttery breath enveloped him.

'Keep open. Try not to blink.'

The drops had dilated his pupils. Now the harness through which the eye-doctor was peering held his chin rigid and pressed on his forehead.

'You can close for a moment.'

Darkness and a vague impression of swimming.

'Open again. Now look up. Down. To the left. Left again. Hold. Now to the right.'

The man's voice was absurdly close, but coming at him as through a rubber tunnel.

'You can relax now.'

The apparatus glided away. Dr Melchiori switched on the overhead light and returned to his roll-top desk. He scribbled. There was a stain on the back of his white coat. It must have been sizeable if he could make it out, for the room was blurred and the letters on the wall-chart quivered and merged.

'It will take a while for the drops to wear off. Be careful when you leave. There are steps. And they're digging up the road. As usual.'

He continued making furious notes and flipped once more through the card on which he had inscribed the measurements taken during the examination.

'I shall prescribe medication. An ointment and drops. To ease the strain. Three times daily. Make sure the drops reach the cornea and the corners of the eye.'

For a moment it sounded like a dismissal and the end of a routine visit. Then the doctor motioned to him to come nearer, to sit not on the narrow metal stool next to the instruments but in the chair by the desk.

'You're not a child. So I had best be frank with you.'

The doctor scrutinized his notes and seemed vexed: Profession: proof-reader, text-editor. 'A trade, my dear sir, not exactly calculated to make things easy for your eyes. How long have you been at it?'

The doctor glanced at his records and nodded.

'More than thirty-five years. As I thought. Why, in heaven's name, did you not come to me before? Why?'

He spun on his chair, aggrieved.

'You say that the morning discomforts, what you call "a burning behind the eyes", began only a few months ago. But why waste even those months? I know: we have waiting lists. The service is overrun. You'll often find me at this desk fifteen or sixteen hours at a stretch. I do realize . . . but in emergencies! When the case is acute. As yours is. I can't hide that from you. I don't hold with baby-talk. Melchiori tells his patients the facts. In plain language.

'There are no miracles. The weakness in the left eye must go back a very long way. Possibly congenital. You did say that your mother wore glasses, didn't you? And you have, my friend, been favouring the right eye far longer, far more intensely than you realize. There was going to be a problem whatever you did. But with your job and this regrettable delay . . .'

Bruno Melchiori looked at him, seeking, soliciting approbation, fiddling with the switch at the base of the desk-lamp. then he turned back to his notes. Exasperated, commiserative.

'The fact is that there is in your left eye little but peripheral vision and that the strain on the right has already caused considerable damage. Considerable. There is a small tear in the retina, just here.'

He thrust a rough sketch across the desk.

'Had you come to me in good time, it would have been worth operating on the left eye. To remove those cataracts. To implant a lens. As matters stand now . . .'

His voice seeped away.

'You are, of course, most welcome to seek a second opinion. Perhaps you should insist on having one. In my judgement, an operation would bring only discomfort and false hopes. The left eye is going on strike, dear sir, on permanent strike. So our real problem is the right.'

The doctor half-turned away, and as to himself: 'Can you change your employment? I didn't think so. What I can do is to give you a medical authorization for a few weeks of leave. The right eye *must* rest. It is infected and must have complete rest. Otherwise ... You do understand me? If you don't give it a rest ...'

The ancient gesture of doleful impotence, palms upward.

'As is, I cannot be too optimistic. Plain words are what I believe in. Your sight will diminish significantly. Whether or not we decide to operate. Whether or not surgery succeeds. The problem with glaucoma and related conditions ... But I won't bore or alarm you with technicalities. As do so many of my esteemed colleagues.'

Melchiori's chin quivered.

'With rest and regular treatment much can be salvaged. But to leave things so late ...'

The nurse, in the swarming corridor of the clinic, helped him impatiently into his coat. When he reached the street, which swam before him in a half-light, he ransacked his pockets for the prescription. But he could not help noticing that the rasp of the tram-car brakes had taken on a new sharpness.

[10]

They gave him a fortnight's leave and tinted glasses. Time turned grey. As if a drowsy wasp were droning and knitting the hours.

He had resolved on method. A touch of physical exercise in the morning (a man's toes, as he bends towards them, can induce melancholy). Three solid hebdomadal sessions at the municipal library, where he would re-read, so as to renew

54

the armoury of his soul, Marx's *Eighteenth Brumaire* – how he remembered the trumpet shock of his first brush with that text. Moreover, there were the newspapers, fanned out on a table at the entrance to the reading-room. With their fat headlines and arresting pictures. The vacuous shelves and bread-lines in Russian cities. The indictment of Party officials in East Germany and Bulgaria. Royalists unfurling banners in Romania. Gorbachev pirouetting for loans and hand-outs in what had been, not long ago, the Escorial of Franco. He read. He thrust the captions close to his right eye as if the Medusa held him fast in her stony smile. And then he sat at the library table, incapable of serious attention.

The winter park was no better. The thinning pigeons seemed to glare at him as if he was a rival for bread-crumbs and peanut shells. The statue of and to Garibaldi, turbaned, his curved blade operatic, with its chiselled promise of emancipation for the common man, struck him as insufferable. He played games with its lapidary syllables, substituting vowels, inverting letters. The resulting obscenities were out of an adolescent's lavatory. A passing couple, tourists, guide-book in hand and muffled against the raw wind, asked him, in halting courtesy, for directions to the Museum of the Resistance. Promptly, loquaciously, he misdirected them. Realizing, as they thankfully departed, that they were Jews, most probably Israelis on some visitation of remembrance. A numbing distaste flooded through him. Against himself, but also against the innocent. As if it was indeed the stiff dolour of the Jews, their inability to let be, which had brought the political and ideological world to its present chaos.

When he told Maura, elaborating the incident in self-reproach, she flinched. Not only then. His constricted emptiness grated on her. She was, just at this time, fiercely over-worked and, he sensed, self-sufficient.

Almost involuntarily, he drifted back to the print-works. Away from the barrens of his supposed rest. His temporary replacement – but was he only that? – tolerated his presence on a cast-off stool in a corner of the eyrie. Let him sit there while he, the young man with the keen glance, scanned the wet pages. The floor quivered to the mallet-strokes of the rotors. One night, the new man vanished to the toilets (a complaisance he had virtually sought to deny himself when total concentration was of the essence). Compulsively, he lifted from the desk one of the sheets, corrected, already initialled and ready to go. He spotted, at once, as if through antennae in his skin, as if with second or third sight exact beyond any in his failing retina, two errors: an accent out of place and a letter in a wrong font. He reached for the red biro.

'For Christ's sake,' breathed the young copy-editor who had returned behind him, cat-like up the metal steps.

'For Christ's sake.'

Not in outright annoyance, but softly, with a hint of derision.

'Nothing escapes the Owl, does it? I've heard all about you. Holding up urgent jobs for a second or third look. The perfectionist.'

He plucked the offending page and laughed outright.

'Do you know what this is? Have you bothered to look? Or don't you read but only proof-read? Have a closer look, *maestro*.'

He thrust the print at him.

'This is a hand-bill. For an auction of used farm implements and manure sacks! To be held in the co-operative of San Maurizio – God knows where that hole is – on Tuesday next. One hundred copies. To be stuck on some outhouse door or dumped in the next ditch. And you worry about an accent!'

'Desperately. Do you know what the Kabbala teaches? That the sum total of the evil and miseries of humankind arose when a lazy or incompetent scribe misheard, took down erroneously, a single letter, one single solitary letter, in Holy Writ. Every horror since has come on us through and because of that one erratum. You didn't know that, did you?'

They faced off in the thumping obscurity and stood speechless as the runner-boy stopped by and scooped up the pile of corrected, imperfect bills.

'You're no help, you know. They haven't dared tell you. The schedules are being tightened. Your sort of practice may suit printers of fine books and copper-plate work. But not here.'

The next packet had just landed on his raked table.

'Not here.'

'On the contrary. It is just here that it matters more than ever before. To act otherwise is utter contempt. Contempt for those who cannot afford to look at a fine book, at quality paper or crafted type. Contempt for those who have a right under God, yes, under God, to have a flawless hand-bill, also for a sale of manure! It is just for those who live in rural holes, in slums, that we should do the best work. So that some spark of perfection will enter their wretched days. Can't you understand, how much contempt there is in a false accent or a misplaced serif? As if you spat at another human being.'

His understudy stared at him. Neutrally. As from some later planet.

'You can sit over there if you want. But let me get on with it.'

And towards the dead hour of first dawn: 'Let me get you some coffee, rabbi.'

He startled at the epithet. He watched embarrassed as his sharer drew back to himself a sheet already initialled and read it a second time.

[11]

His hand loitered on her buttock. The tremor in his wrist came and went.

'Not to worry,' said Maura.

Would she say next: 'It can happen'?

She did and his insides knotted. She veered towards him and brushed his cheeks with her lips. He reached for his unaccustomed spectacles on the night-table. The one lens might, for all the difference it made, be window glass. The other was so thick that, had anyone bothered to take notice, it was not an owl they would compare him to but a frog, bulbous-eyed and groping. Maura sought to draw him back to her, gently. But the stale inside him continued shaking, like a minor bog.

'Nerves,' she offered.

He peered at the rain-sodden streak of early light under the edge of the blinds. He had woken dimly out of a punishing dream, but erect and reaching for Maura's warm back. She had nestled close. Then nothing. The branch sagging under some dead weight. Nothing. She cradled the deadness in her hand, consoling. He wanted to rip her touch away, but held the rage and the ache in his throat. And fought for breath. 'This room, the mausoleum.' The phrase chimed out of the ebbing dream. Then he made the connection.

Television, the slow killer. They had watched the mid-night news round-up and review of the week. Naked under the partial tent of the bed cover. The re-consecration of Saint Basil's Cathedral on Red Square, with its onion-bulb cupolas and Lego-set minarets and the splotches of gold-leaf pillaged from the ancient Khans. The bells were whipping the pigeons and swifts to a frenzy. Across the square wound a slow procession of the faithful, cradling candles. The camera, inside the nave, lingered on the upturned visages, the brimming eyes and clasped hands of the worshippers. It panned across their mouths, slack with ecstasy and a queer sort of greed. Greed for rememberance, for homecoming, for the annulment of time (seventy years, was it?).

'Look at their faces. I've seen faces like that before. In medical encyclopaedias. The happy faces of imbeciles. Of the senile.'

She had not answered and he felt mired in the morass of his outrage.

'Just look: the rolling eyes of cretins, the wet mouths. There has never been any church more corrupt, more servile. None that has been a blacker censor of truth and free thought.'

The candles seemed to gather the chant and the fug of incense and the ardent breaths into a single pyre.

Why had he not turned the thing off?

On came the commentator. A woman star in the television firmament. Brushing a tear from her lighthouse eyes. 'After the long and terrifying night, after more than two genera-tions. Treasured viewers, my friends, join me at this historic hour, here on the steps of Saint Basil's in Moscow. The Eucharist. Once again. Bread for the starved hearts. Who never lost hope. Never. And now we can share in their felicity. Look, just look at the light on the gilt domes. And now . . .' A dramatic cut as the cameras swung abruptly towards a squat, lightless shape barely distinguishable under the Kremlin walls. 'Lenin's tomb.' Her voice was honeyed with victory. 'That famous, or ought we to say infamous, mausoleum. How much longer till it is shut, till the waxen figure of the despot is removed?'

After Maura had switched off the set, sleep stayed out of reach. When it came, so did the sour dreams, the flotsam of nightmare. Maura got out of bed and slipped into her bathrobe. Recently, still, its ochre and autumn-leaf pattern had moved him almost to grateful tears. Now he observed the rent at the hem and the hurried patching. He took in the cough and hiss of the toilet. He felt broken, the air knocked out of him. Maura rolled up the blinds and lit the gas-range. He tugged at himself with gross effort. The numbness eased. But staring at his naked legs as he put his feet on the scrap of rug at the foot of the bed, he suffered a sense of utmost strangeness, perceiving his feet not as his own but, through the layers of the lens, as belonging to some intimate unknown. To someone under way towards him.

[12]

The start of the meeting lacked elevation. Cesare Lombardi turned aggressively to the matter of dues. Had the treasurer, he demanded, taken into account the fact, 'the manifest fact', as he put it on a note of stentorian reproach, that any long-term adjournment, let alone dissolution of the Circle of Marxist Revolutionary Theory and Praxis would necessitate – his voice underlined that hallowed word – the reimbursement of some equitable portion of the membership fees and of the subscription to both the cyclostyled Bulletin and the complete works of Plekhanov to which the *Circolo* had so imprudently (surely, members recalled his, Cesare's cautionary dissent) committed itself?

The treasurer, one Alberto P., with a tendency to slide into a mild stupor during theoretical debates, fumbled at his notes, snapped the rubber bands and inserted a paperclip in his mouth.

He was, opined Alberto, not altogether confident that there was anything left over in the kitty. Not after the summer outing and the replacement of the broken chair, which the school where they convened had insisted on. As to the further tomes of Plekhanov (the frayed prospectus fell to the floor), he would do his best, but harboured some blurred apprehension that the *casa editrice*, the publishing house for Workers' Higher Schooling responsible for that monumental undertaking, had itself gone into recent liquidation.

Tullio laughed under his breath. But audibly. Which did not help.

Anna B.'s anguish bore on the minutes of past gatherings. These were, assuredly, of historical 'and ethical' – she stressed the addendum – import. An act of witness, a testimonial whose status would not be effaced (at which point her pudgy hands managed a gesture of peculiar desolation) by the grievous change in the fortunes of the movement. 'The movement', the way she breathed the phrase made it plain that it was not the nine members of the Circle actually present tonight, but a vast throng progressing out of time, out of perennial enslavements, the Spartacus revolt, the peasant rebellions and millenarian uprisings, the Communards and the innocent and the kneeling shot down on that grand square in Saint Petersburg in 1905, a column without end of the mutinous and the vanquished, giving their lives to the cause, in 1917, in the cellars of Shanghai and torture chambers of Madrid, Berlin, Santiago, singing to stay awake in the frozen inferno of Stalingrad, unquenchable then, unquenchable tomorrow. 'The movement'. To which, humble as they might be, the minutes, the chronicles of the Circle belonged.

As spoken by a somnambulist, with the faintest accent of resurrection.

But there was another side to the coin.

'One must be practical.'

Comrade Anna drove her thumb into her palm.

'Comrades will acknowledge that I have always attended to practicalities.'

No dissent from that.

'Suppose our minutes were to fall into the wrong hands. Is it not likely, indeed almost certain, that Fascism will re-emerge from the present crisis?'

Her alarm swept the room.

'Fascism in its most ruthless, mechanized and avenging guise? Aided, financed by American intelligence and the renegades scurrying across from the east. In which event there will be blacklists. Just as when Mussolini's hooligans took over. House to house. The night-visitors with their rolls of names, their truncheons and their castor oil. If the minutes of the CMRTP were to be found, everyone associated with it would be hunted down and imprisoned.'

She hovered over the prospect with some fascination.

'A clandestine organization, and that is what we will have to become, must keep no records, it must leave no betraying spoors. See Lenin, 1902. Am I right, *Professore*? We must find a truly safe hiding-place. The Fascist and the CIA pigs could nose out truffles buried deep.'

(The simile was not hers.)

But in self-conscious unison the members present murmured the shibboleth: 'What then is to be done?'

It was Father Carlo who struck the higher note. Was there not, he asked, a difference between the dissolution of the group, as it figured on tonight's order of business, and its cessation?

Let him explain. His training in dogma and church history had left him with an awed intimation of the paradigm of the king's 'two bodies'. The king's mortal flesh could die. But the incarnate identity, the essence of royalty, could not. It inhered, intact, materially immortal in the crowned effigy placed either on a special pediment or on the throne itself, an *imago* of a real presence to which courtiers brought daily news and food and drink till the new monarch was proclaimed. By virtue of which usage, the continuity of the institution of kingship was guaranteed. Dissolution would abolish the Circle and pronounce it defunct. Resignation of its several members – did they not see the close analogy to the royal case? – resignation for whatever reason, would ensure its survival. He was not urging a sophism or arcane paradox. An organization could endure even if, temporarily, no one chose to adhere to it. Wells dry up and the deep springs return again. Who knows what may lie ahead after this present quake?

A query which impelled even Tullio to turn towards the *Professore*.

Father Carlo's allegory had greatly moved and persuaded him. There can be no 'dissolution of a truth', of any fundamental order of human insight and proven discovery. No tearing down of a wall, no overthrow of a regime, not even the collapse of the USSR, could refute the verities shared by those whom he now addressed. On the contrary. A new phase of imperialist exploitation, racism and wage slavery, in short, an Americanization of the planet, would attest to the unshakeable foresight of Marxist theory. Short, even middle-term prognostications had gone wrong. There was no use denying that. Capitalism had not only survived the two world wars which it had caused, it had not only weathered cyclical depressions, but had turned these to its profit. Members had, he trusted, read Hobsbawm's analysis in the last but one issue of the Bulletin. Keynes, a figure of sinister genius, had appropriated certain Marxist techniques in order to rescue capitalism from ruin. The condition of the working classes *had* improved.

At which concession, Comrade Anna shrugged grimly.

'Why shut one's eyes to that or to Marx's error concerning the ineluctable pauperization of the proletariat? No nineteenth-century mind, however capacious, could anticipate either the exponential benefits capitalism would harvest from its investment in research and development, in high technology, or the inability of the underdeveloped world to resist expropriation and insurmountable debt.'

This did *not* mean that Marxist revolutionary theory had been disproved or made obsolete. The exact opposite was the case. That theory needed to be deepened and made more flexible. It seemed to him perfectly obvious that major conflicts lay ahead: between Islam and the west, between the northern and the southern hemispheres, between inflationary capital and the debt-structure on which it cynically depended. North America was entering an accelerating spiral of recessions and bank-failures. Never had there been more need of theoretical clarity.

It might be that migrant labour would swamp western Europe. What then? To dissolve their Circle would be folly. The day would come when its membership would no longer total twenty or a dozen but hundreds and thousands thereafter!

His ardour had fallen flat. Nods all around, to be sure. And Anna put an awkward hand on his shoulder. But Tullio's 'speaking concretely' seemed immediate and undeniable.

'Speaking concretely', Tullio failed to see much use in further convocations. Even free copies of their Bulletin found no takers. The attempt to organize a workshop plus picnic in the housing estates or among the senior classes in the schools and polytechnics had aborted dismally. Humiliation seemed to lie like salt on Tullio's tongue. To him, also, Marxism was, at signal points, the truth. But not true just now. Not in the actual situation in which men and women, and not only capitalist profiteers and neo-Fascist gangsters, were living their lives. A dry season, as the *Monsignore* had so neatly put it.

'Why, then, spit in the empty well?'

Tullio had concluded. Adjournment *sine die*. A vote of thanks to the relieved treasurer (Lombardi abstaining). Maura would let the school know that the room would, for the time being, no longer be thankfully required. The *Professore* would undertake to keep the records in a safe place. Anna's mien registered doubt. Was there any further business?

They stood up. Still vexed. Lombardi knocked over his chair. Was it Maura who intoned first, in a low, trained voice? 'Arise ye prisoners of starvation . . .' They joined hands, embarrassed. The rhetoric brought pain. But he sang. Out of tune. And this time Maura's smile to him was like warm bread.

As they unravelled, heading in different directions, Anna B. looked back and raised her fist in . . . He was going to say 'valediction'. That would have been another erratum. She raised it in promise and in terror.

[13]

He had taken the trip on an impulse. Probably ill-considered. Even the special excursion fare to Rome intended, he wryly noted, for pilgrims in quest of remission and absolution at the holy places, sapped his budget – one now stretched·to the limit because he knew he would only be able to resume his proof-readings part-time, if at all. It was a loan from Tullio which had made possible his overnight stay in a grotty *pensione* near the railway station. Dutiful but hurried hands had assisted him down the steep steps from the carriage to the platform. He was on his own in the blaring rush of the city. As a child, he had rubbed his eyeballs to provoke crystalline star-showers. Cleaning his glasses obsessively, blinking hard, all he could produce now was an undulant mist.

He knew Rome's orange-grey and the smoky light which gave to many of its monumentalities their ghostly weight. On a much earlier visit, he had been made uneasy by the mottled air and the sepia wash which lay, day in and day out, on the august walls and arches. But this time the dun veil, which floated between himself and the illustrious sites, hung within. He walked slowly, hesitated at corners and picked at railings.

The nastiness had been reported, very briefly, at the bottom of a column of miscellaneous crimes in the national press. The plaque in the Street of the Dark Shops in Rome had been vandalized by unknown, though presmably neo-Fascist or royalist defacers.

*

He remembered how he had found that plaque, years ago, and how he had deposited, at the feet of the wall, a small bunch of violets. The event commemorated was one among hundreds no less atrocious enacted on those antique streets and squares between 1943 and liberation. Fifteen members of a Communist underground resistance group had been betrayed into the hands of the Waffen SS by an elderly, observant housekeeper prone to insomnia. They had been tortured. So far as could be discovered, not one had broken and given up further names. Not the sixteen-year-old boy whose testicles they had put in a carpenter's vice. Not the three young women whose bodies had been chequered with cigarette burns. Not the old man (the name suggested that he was a Jew) whose beard they had torn out hair by hair and whose hands they inserted in a door-jamb. They then had dragged their prisoners to the narrow street, propped them against the wall and machine-gunned them. One of the victims, his legs smashed during interrogation, had slipped to his knees when the SS opened fire. Seeing him alive, they kicked him to death, slowly. For years, it was said, the runnels and star-splashes of human blood could be made out like fading burns on the stone.

Standing in front of the inscription on his visit long ago, testing its lettering and the incision of the Party badge, he had, almost unawares, committed to memory a number of the names. Bartani (Adriana). Pradone (Vigilio) – the boy. Gildo (Manuele). Together with their dates of birth. Comrades. Rostagni (Marco), aged twenty-three when they strapped him to the table. Condini (Fabio), the leader of the cell who had, on the very eve of the war, published in a clandestine edition that notable essay on Marx's reading of Lucretius. Comrades in arms about whose courage and sacrifice there could be no question and whose doomed faith and actions had cleansed Rome of some part of its unholiness, of its self-betrayals.

Encasing these names in his memory, adverting to them on occasion, he imagined he was practising something like the Jewish rite of *kaddish*. The refusal to forget, to let death have the final say over lives which must remain living.

He was not alone. A small group had gathered in the Botteghe Oscure. The memorial had not only been smeared with the double-lightning of the SS across a star of David ludicrously misshapen, but part of the marble had also been chipped away, and a rough fissure now sliced through the column of names. Those assembled, they amounted to perhaps a dozen, stared at the damage. One or two had brought fresh flowers. These lay at the rim of the gutter amid the splinters of rent stone and the dribble of brown paint. The right brown, he noted, that of the shirts.

A very old man was shaking helplessly, his sobs out of control. He managed the name of Santori (Anna Maria).

'She was my sister. My sister. They raped her first. She kept saying "Stalingrad". So they tore out her teeth. Anna Maria. I am Giuseppe Santori.'

He turned to the bystanders for confirmation.

A tall man in a sheepskin jacket, the collar raised, said: 'Bastards. Fascist bastards.' And walked off abruptly.

It was the woman just in front of him, long motionless, who turned and spoke to him.

'Now they are going to change the name of the Party. I call that spitting on the dead. Doing dirt on them greater than this. We expect this sort of shit from the Fascist swine. But now it is the Party . . . Forgive my language: pissing on history.'

She had steeled herself to say the word aloud and carried on more freely.

'My mother was one of them. She happened to be away carrying messages to the partisans in Orvieto when the SS came. Otherwise . . .'

She looked at the stained names.

'She knew who betrayed them. The foul bitch died only a few years ago. In a cosy home for the aged. Paid for by your and my taxes, *Signore*.'

The laugh was forced.

'My mother unearthed her not long after the Americans came. She wanted to have her arrested and put away. I imagine she was even ready to kill her. But the hag cringed and whined and offered Mother bits of hideous jewellery and money. Mother vomited and left her blubbering on the floor. But the Party is no better. It is betraying them all over again. I can wager that they would rather not replace the plaque. So embarrassing. Men and women done to death with the names of Togliatti, of Stalin, yes of Stalin, in their hearts.'

She shut her lips tight and turned away. He saw the slow shiver of anger and disgust pass through her shoulders. Now her back trembled. His hand was on her arm. She did not remove it but drew it more closely to her when she saw him fumbling at the edge of the steps which led to the piazza. She was, he decided, beautiful.

In the diminutive trattoria confidence flowed easily. They had agreed to share the bill, but the thin wine, he insisted, was to be on his side of the ledger. She sold plastic and fake-leather bags, belts, gloves, accessories and costume bangles in a boutique behind Via Veneto. At first, she kept eyeing her watch. Then, with shy bravado and over a second cup of coffee, she announced that she was taking the afternoon off. Let them dock her wretched pay if they chose.

She detested the job anyway; the odour of celluloid and varnish, the customers pawing the goods endlessly and then complaining about their own finger-marks on the fabric.

Yes, she would take today off. In homage to the defiled dead. How her mother had feared and scorned shop-keepers, she who had been an educated woman but tubercular.

Her own existence? Quickly inventoried. A father who escaped, as into air, soon after her birth. Trade-school. The years as a receptionist in a garage and repair-yard on the road to Ostia. Oh, indeed, quite close to the one in which Pasolini had been attacked. Then, a shadow in her left lung. A less taxing employment, or so it sounded, in diverse emporia and boutiques.

No, it had not worked out. The man was of some intelligence and political decency, but restless. They had parted more or less amicably. The first few postcards had come from Tunis. Then nothing. Yes (and she was at ease reporting it), there had been episodes since. But something in the incompletion of her ways – the phrase intrigued him – seemed to exclude others. Or it might be, and her smile quickened the light all around her, that those who came too near to her, to these incompletions and jagged edges, felt – how should she put it? – superfluous or scratched. At this image she reddened and laughed into her wine.

But what of him?

When they got up, the trattoria had emptied, and the waiter was wiping neighbouring tables with palpable reproof.

Nothing like it had ever happened to him before.

With its unspoken self-evidence.

He did not recall their progress through immaterial streets, only the firm tug of her arm as she conducted him across loud tram-rails, around ruts and steep pavements. Nor did he really remember their ascent in the clanging lift. What was vivid to his recollection was her low warm laugh as she fumbled at her key-ring and failed, twice, to use the right key to open her own door. They undressed each other like children in a lost game. Her lips sped across his whole body and lingered where it was worn. The loveliness of her arched back pierced him with wonder. His fingers idled in her unpinned hair as she knelt. When he entered her and let that high soundless wave carry him, a single word rang in his unbound being: 'dormition'. He had read it in a catalogue of old masters and did not know quite what it meant. Not so he could define it. But in that motion towards and with her, dormition seemed to signify a waking sleep, a peace and rest so whole as to be on the other side, on the lit and southern side of sleep.

In the darkening afternoon they spoke of this and that. In abbreviated yet long-familiar phrases. It was only when putting on his clothes that he noticed the stack of cuttings and pamphlets on her dresser. Horoscopes, astrological charts, predictions of planetary conjunctions to come and of their portent. She beamed at him full of confident zeal.

What, exactly, were the hour and the day of his nativity? She would read his palm for that also was a science of which she had some knowledge. The desecration they had witnessed that morning and which had brought them together, Taurus and Libra, had been foretold. That is why she had turned to him so naturally. No less foreseeable was the return of the Communist Party to repute and power. When Jupiter and enigmatic Neptune were in the house of the Lion. There could be no shadow of doubt. Not for those who would see. Once baleful Saturn had moved out of Scorpio . . .

She reached for a tract and pressed it on him. What had
been his mother's astral sign, her favourite precious stone?

'Tell me, please.'

They parted strangers, and he hurried to the station.

[14]

He was walking too fast. Twice already, he had come up hard
against edges and breaks in the pavement. Now his feet
caught in a discarded carrier-bag, its garish design malig-
nantly alive in the wind. He kicked blindly at the thing.

A sentence sprayed on the back of the bus-stop shelter
seized his notice. 'God does not believe in God.'

To which a lesser hand, armed only with red chalk, had
added the word *our*: 'God does not believe in our God.'

Absurdly, a touch of fear stung him, and the momentary,
deranged conviction that a deserted universe, like a house
unlocked after the removal vans had gone, would sink into
oblivion if he failed to carry out his present purpose. He felt
the inane certitude that this enactment, so trivial in itself, was
the litany of which Father Carlo had once told him, whose
recitation, out of however gutted and reduced a human
mouth and soul, kept reality going and coerced the tired
future into its advent.

Shivering in the cold, he wiped his glasses and pressed on.

Though he knew his city well, the building was not easy to
find. Instead of the customary name-plate by the entrance, he
was able to make out only a bent card, illegibly inscribed, and
pinned to the down-stairs letter box. The stairs lay in thick
shadow and he groped uselessly for the light-switch. At the
fifth landing, he found the door closed. He pulled at the bell.
The sound came back muffled and distant. He pulled again

and waited. He was about to reverse his steps when the door inched open. He could not really see the figure behind the crack.

What was it he wanted?

He stated his intention.

If anything, the opening narrowed even more.

Was he a practical joker? A provocateur?

Urgently he leaned against the door handle.

'Nothing of the kind!'

He advanced his name, the date of his original adherence, the number on his Party card. He inventoried his Party assignments and activities.

Was he babbling? The sad notion crossed his mind.

He cited the names of several comrades who could vouch for him, who knew of his purposed recantation.

A muted, theatrical laugh on the other side of the door. But the opening widened.

Innerly, to be perfectly honest, he had never left the Party. He had only sought to clear up for himself, at a time of especial internal contradictions, some theoretical conundra (it was too late to rescind that pretentious, evasive word). Certain perplexities which had also troubled other comrades. He had been wrong. He knew that now. As Bukharin had taught: deviants, however right *subjectively*, belong to the limbo of history.

Again the miserly laugh. But the door opened.

The man was in slippers and a smell of fish clung to his sweater. A pan – soup, coffee? – was spluttering behind a curtained recess. Parallel to the door, as in a second line of defence, stood a table. Printed forms, roneoed sheets, cigarette ash. Now he saw that the man held an unlit cigarette between his lips.

'You *are* a queer one, aren't you, *Professore*. Isn't that what

73

they called you? Always talking. Talk, talk. If you ask me, that's where we made our big mistake. There's no pay-off in talk. Take to the streets. Smash their fucking skulls. Occupy the factories. That's what I always said.'

The surly recognition, the recall of his mocking sobriquet, filled him with rare joy. He was eager to debate the issue, to identify the leftist infantilism (Lenin's decisive tag) of the man's position. But he checked himself and asked with humility whether he could apply for reinstatement.

'Haven't you heard?'

The man motioned towards a scatter of cards half-hidden under a file at one end of the table.

'Those are just this past week's. Most tear up their Party cards or stuff them in the incinerator. But some do send theirs. With obscenities attached. Shall I read them to you, Comrade?'

That would not be necessary, and he heard the irony in the mode of address. Yet he flushed with contentment.

'By next month, honoured sir, there may not be a Party.'

Ah, but there would be, leaner, more astringent, better armed theoretically. The truth knows no circumstance. Tullio was wrong. If God no longer believed in God, the time had come for man to believe in man. Only Marxism could make that belief effective.

The functionary cut him off with a shrug. He drew a creased form from one of the piles and nudged it across the table. An application for membership. He would pass it on to the committee. Which had not, in weeks, succeeded in assembling a quorum. There was a small fee for processing.

He had the notes ready. The man counted them and considered him with distaste.

'The Party will examine your case. And that's what you must be, believe me. A case.'

The lame play on words seemed to trigger silent mirth. He shook his head.

'You'll hear from us.'

Then he looked down at the form which the applicant had begun to fill in.

'Don't you even read a paper? Haven't you heard? "I hereby apply for acceptance in the Communist Party." There is no such thing, my friend! There is no more PCI. *Basta. Finito.*'

Detaching each funeral syllable, he slid the flat of his hand across his wind-pipe.

'Gone and buried, the old whore. It is now the Party of the Democratic Left.'

He spelled out the new initials hoarsely.

'No more red star. A green tree. Look here: a bushy green tree.'

He waved the new logo in front of the *Professore*'s face.

'Is that what you want to join? Well, is it?'

It was. So precisely that the penitent could find no rejoinder, no words for his thirst. Only a puppet's quick unseeing nod.

The man cleared his throat impatiently, spat into a grey handkerchief and bade him write his address. In capital letters, if you please.

He would be receiving a summons from the district committee.

'Though only God knows when.'

God did seem much about in the city these days. So be it. The real battle with Him lay ahead.

The door shut loudly.

It was only at the bottom of the stair-well, still in pitch blackness, that he realized he had not held on to the banister. Not even once. But then one doesn't need to, does one, when coming home.

75

DESERT ISLAND DISCS

His requests did stretch the resources, almost all-encompassing, of the sound-archive. But that is part of the game.

First he asked to hear Fortinbras's belch. The one at the end of the interminable coronation carouse. There was no use denying it: despite tireless scrubbing, new rushes on the floor of the hall, the aromatic salts expended on the long tables and logs in the chimney, the death smells persisted. They hung sweet and rancid in the corners and by the tower stairs. There had been too many corpses. Was it six, was it seven? Fortinbras the King found it hard to remember. A woman's carrion among them, bloated and waxen, with the scent of burnt almonds on her twisted lips. The surviving folk, royal cousins and courtiers, had been pleasant enough. Caps lifted, knees bent to the new monarch. General sentiments of relief. And now the King's chambers were being thoroughly aired, the arras taken down and replaced by more cheerful hangings. Still, the feast had not been unblemished. There was the thin, faintly hysterical child on the balcony, troubling the military fanfare – plain lads out of Norway, not those Danish luteners and players on elaborate pipes, most of whom had, anyway, taken to their heels at the first cannon shot. Flitting among them in her pale, nearly transparent gown. A younger sister, or so the King had been informed, of one Ophelia, drowned. And there was the good Horatio, solemn as a blind horse. Assuring the new sovereign of his insightful fidelity, of his imminent retirement, telling him that the great and dread events of which he, Horatio, had been humble witness, must be memorably noted. Horatio to Fortinbras, in a hushed, dulcet tone; the King having to strain his battle-deafened ears to catch the man's desolate, incessant drift.

The wines had been heavy, and the herring. Dawn could not be far off. Even through the thick walls and battlements, Fortinbras the son of Norway could sense the changing rasp of the sea when dawn approaches. He was bone-tired. Almost envious of the dead prince, who had always seemed to him like a master of sleep, and of the secrets which sleep breeds. Fortinbras belched. It was a loud, cavernous belch. From the inmost of his drowsing, armoured flesh. It was a sound the courtiers would not forget. Thunderous and replete with the promise of a simpler tomorrow.

The second recording he asked for was that of the neighing of the little horse, of the dappled grey with the cropped right ear, after it had cantered into the surrounding hills.

The journey had been hot and dust-choked. The ticks and the blue flies hammered like mad that long day. They had left the high gates and the cobbles of the town well before sunrise. But even at that hour, the air had been listless and the heat trapped underfoot. And there had been a strange unrest in the courtyard. The old woman with the pale eyes and heavy brooch had exuded a kind of quivering. The dappled had felt it in his wet nostrils: night-sweat and spilled seed. Not that the actual trip was of any danger or difficulty. They had made it often. Past the spring with its loud bucket, through the olive groves and into the baking plain. Then onward to where gaps in the burnt hills flashed with the sheen of the gulf. The old master was light in his cart and the driver scarcely more than a rude, overbearing teenager. The horse had heard him in the stables, boasting of his manhood, of his prowess with the whip, of the leaves he chewed and of the hot dreams they brought on. But the voyage should have been routine, and the shaft-horse, though patronizing (he had been to the oracle before the grey was foaled), was friendly enough.

It all happened at such speed. The horses had been half-asleep, their eyes closed against the damned flies. Out of breath with the heat and the slight rise which leads to the place where the three roads meet, the two slaves were trotting in the spare shade of the cart. The old man was humming to himself, as he often did, a lullaby to a new-born child, but breaking off, always, as on a jagged tooth. Then the harsh pull on the reins, forcing the horses almost to their haunches. The slash of the whip and the charioteer's high-pitched obscenities. The muffled call of the old man, his bony arms waving in the drumming air. And cutting through it all, a voice which the dappled would never shake out of its ears. A voice strangely like his old master's, but totally different: raw yet resonant, like that of a bronze clarion. A call so brimful of rage that it tore the skin off one's back, but knowing, with a knowledge that was like a knife.

One of the windmill strokes from the traveller's knotted staff grazed the little horse's neck. It was not a direct blow – he had heard the old man's skull crack and the death-rattle of the driver – but of a contemptuous violence. The traces had snapped like dry reeds and the grey had raced for the hills. The sharp flint had galled his hoofs and now, at sunset, the shadows ran cold. Looking back, the little horse had glimpsed a figure running desperately towards Thebes. Was it one of the slaves, or the traveller? He did not know. And began neighing, uncertain of his fodder.

His third record request was for the scratch or, more precisely, for the sibilant swerve (in G minor) of the steel nib on Rudolf Julius Emmanuel Clausius's pen in the instant in which this pen wrote the n in the exponential n minus x to the nth power in the equation of entropy.

Würzburg is not, even at its best, an ebullient town. On that early spring evening in 1863, the rain was streaming down the grimed windows. His lids heavy, Herr Clausius blinked and bent closer to his work-table. A grey film seemed to hang around the gas-lamp, and when the draughts streaked through the curtains, the china globe of the lamp shivered morosely. Clausius observed with annoyance that these same gusts made his dentures throb. Unnoticing he pressed the pen-holder against his aching molar. Foxed with the damp, the off-prints of Sir William Thomson's papers on thermodynamics and Sadi Carnot's *mémoire* on the airpump lay at his elbow. Carnot's two equations, for the boiler when the piston was in position a, and when it was in position a prime, hummed, as it were, at the enervated edge of Clausius's awareness. Like two stick-insects, their brittle feelers interlocked. Somewhere in the house, and behind the splattering rain, a clock chimed and rattled. Konstanze had, again, forgotten to wind it.

To the nth power. The nib hovered over the paper, and for an idle moment Clausius's attention wandered, through the armorial and dragon-maze of the watermark. The equation stood. Against reason. Against the long-drawn breath of life. In uncaring defiance of the future tense. Formally, the algebra was nothing but the proof, at once abstract and statistical, of the unrecuperability of caloric energy when turned to heat, of the degree of loss in all thermal and thermodynamic processes. That is how Clausius would entitle and describe his paper when dispatching it to the *acta* of the Prussian Academy of Science (Section IV: Applied Science). But what he was staring at – and the sensation was rather more distant, more indifferent than that of his bruised gums – was the determination, irrefutable, of the heat-death of the universe. The n minus x function would not be bought off. Entropy meant run-down and the transmutation of spent energy into cold stasis. A stillness, a cold past all imagining. Compared to which our own deaths and the decomposition of the warm flesh are a trivial carnival. In that equation, the cosmos had its epitaph. In the beginning was the Word; at the close was the algebraic function. A pen-nib, bought in a scrolled cardboard box at Kreutzner's, university stationer, had put *finis* to the sum and total of being. After the downward right-hand stroke of that n came not infinite blackness, which *is* still, but a nothingness, an unfathomable zero. Unthinking, Clausius started tracing a line beneath the equation. But the nib had gone dry.

The custodians of the sound-archive are not prudish. They know how often hearing is overhearing, and brought him his fourth disc unblinking.

A petty nightmare of a day. The first flight cancelled at Brussels Airport because of a work-to-rule by French air-controllers. Planes stacked over Europe like stale rusks in holding patterns and the fog thickening. He had rung her apartment; she must have left minutes before. Which meant she was already at the railway terminal. His change ran out as he tried to reach the station and have her paged on the public address system (knowing how incensed she would be at the grossness of hearing her name loud-hailed, though it was a coded sobriquet, he was almost glad he had not succeeded). As through cotton wool, he heard the announcement of a possible departure to L. from the other terminal. He bounded awkwardly along the escalator and connecting tunnel, only to find a dozen other stranded passengers at the stand-by counter. When he finally took off, it was late

83

afternoon. The hotel room had been booked in an assumed though, God knows, transparent name and she would not be able to claim the reservation. Would she have the spend-thrift nonchalance to take another room in the same hotel? She would bridle at that.

With the fog slow to lift, the airport at L. was teeming and the lines at the passport-window interminable. He reached the hotel almost hysterical with exasperation and guilt. No sign of her. He lacked the nerve to inquire whether a lady of singular radiance (or so she was to him) had left her overnight bag with the *portier*.

The streets and squares of the city were awash with taw-dry snow and patches of black ice. The flicker of neon lights dazzled him as it bounced off the tramcar-rails and shop windows. He circled aimlessly, back to the hotel lobby. Once more across the gusting bridge. Now obliquely and towards the cold flatness of the lake. He detested the place. He had loved it beyond words when last they had arrived there, the lights of the station underpass caught in her live hair. Now towards the hotel again, his hands trembling.

He found her. At the bottom of the unlit alley below the steps to the old town. She heard him running and turned. They stumbled, like drunks, into the solid dark of an arched doorway.

The sounds came in a soft rush. That of her fingers in his perspiring hair as he knelt. Of the buttons slipping out of the braided hooks of her long coat. The rustle of her skirt, like the leafy edge of summer, as she drew it up her thighs. And when his tongue came home to her, from above his dizzied head and shoulders, that laugh, distant at first, over-arching, then closer than his own skin. The hushed chime of her laugh (it was this he had requested from the

84

archive) as he drank of her. A note which left his soul singing and crazy with peace.

There is, so far as is known, only one (and imperfect) tape extant of the otherwise lost Trio in F Major for crumhorn, double bass and Sumatran conch-bells which Sigbert Weimerschlund composed in the year of his death. The choice of instruments, though perhaps *recherché*, had seemed to Weimerschlund inevitable. As deputy curator of the palaeontology collection in the Atheneum in Second Falls (Ohio), he had long been spellbound by the serpentine, delicately rifled contours of certain immemorially ancient horned beasties. His heart attack in the cruel winter of 1937 – a serious hiccup, some years later, was to cause his decease – had left Weimerschlund with a singular aural vestige. At certain moments, in the face of a prairie wind, under professional stress – the Second Falls Chamber of Commerce, though sympathetic, recurrently put in question the value of the Atheneum and, more especially, of its fossil cabinets, which the new Estes Polk Memorial High School was, in any event, prepared to house – or when sheer lonesome gluttony had seduced him into bringing to his boarding-house room and consuming at one go a whole quarter-pound of chopped herring, Weimerschlund would hear, inside the echo-chamber of his ventricles, a low syncopated thrumming. A dense beat, a second beat echoing the first, then a vibrato. Tremolo and reprise sounding from the shadow-left of his heart. Though alarming, the sequence had its eerie charm, and Sigbert sometimes found himself hesitant to reach for the assuaging pills. Hence, after the crumhorn, the double bass.

The conch-bells, not bells really but nacreous, iridescent sea-shells suspended on a bamboo frame and graduated according to the pentatonic scale, did, he knew, represent an extravagant touch. Weimerschlund had never, of course, been anywhere in range of Sumatra. But he had heard the chiming glitter, the sea-arpeggios of conch-bells through a tent-wall on the night when Hubbard's Circus and Raree Show had stopped in Second Falls. Weimerschlund scarcely remembered what improbable impulse had taken him to the fairground. He fled in nausea from the eyes of the caged timber-wolf and the cackle of the pink-haired Tom Thumb. Looking for an exit, he heard that crystal scale; as if the wind had made the snow sing. Riveted, he pressed his ear to the muting canvas. He squirmed still at the recollection of his indiscreet gesture: Sigbert Weimerschlund, deputy curator and Shriner, down on all fours, prizing loose the sodden tent-flap to peer inside. Where he glimpsed, by the sheen of a greying light-bulb, only the back of the player. It was, he later thought, the back of a boy or very young man (The Indian Rope-Trick Performed by Tamu the Blind Pearl Diver).

The precise circumstances under which the Trio had been recorded by the three brothers – he was now listening to a tape taken from the 78 – are a matter of mild musicological dispute. Nor should one advance exaggerated claims for the quality of the piece. It is, after all, amateur work. Weimerschlund appears to have overlooked that *pizzicati* on a double bass produce awkward effects when in counterpoint to the nasal register of the crumhorn. No, what remains memorable is the devoted performance. Zeppo manages to draw from the crumhorn not its customary sedate buzz, but a desolate and oracular hum. His breath-control, his variations of pitch and flutter, are those of a virtuoso. On the double bass, Harpo has lapses. It is not he, however, who is to blame when Weimerschlund calls for a *glissando* at the start of the last movement and, unreasonably, marks it *presto*. In Chico's hands or, more accurately, under the felt mallet as Chico wields it, the Sumatran chimes are magic. It is they who prelude, by means of a subtle *rubato*, the transcendent moment in the Trio: the return to the dominant, nineteen bars from the close. A moment in which the ache of the horn, the heart-thrum of the double bass, itself like a footfall on a winter path, are fused by the almost imperceptible yet rhythmically binding flicker of the bells. This, he fancied, as he listened in the studio, might well be the music played, and these the performers, in the waiting-room for the Last Judgement.

The painting which occasioned his sixth and final selection is little known. An unreliable mimeographed check-list is all that is made available, morosely, by the semi-private collection in the French Savoie in which it is hung. Labelled 'By the Master of the Chambéry Passion', it is a Crucifixion on gilded panelling which can most plausibly be dated mid-fourteenth century and ascribed to one of the workshops in the Turin area. The taut, angular grouping with St Damian at the edge, the motif of crossed lances and gonfalons against a dullish burnt-earth background and empty sky, suggest the influence either of Baldassare Ordosso himself or of one of his apprentices (a number of these are known to have journeyed the Alps into France after 1345). The torn features of Christ, the somewhat rhetorical gesture of the Mother of God – observe her heightened knuckles and the touch of sweat around her azure head-band – are well executed but iconographically routine.

It is the red-headed lad in the attendant crowd, the fourth figure from the left, who arrests attention. He is whistling.

On two supple fingers inserted, shepherd- or street-urchin-style, into a corner of his full lips. Whistling, either to himself or to some listener – a crony, a sheep-dog, a girl – outside the scene. There can be no mistake. The whistle is a loud and joyous one, as of a thrush on a spring upland. The whistler's firm, green-hosed legs tell us that, as does the merry swelling of his throat and cheeks. And though his lips are pursed, there can be no doubt as to the smile and dawn cheer which gives them breath. Yet the young man's eyes are on the Cross, on the twisted flesh and the petals of bright blood around the nails. The eyes are unwavering as he whistles, as the pure clear merriment rises into the paschal air.

What he asked for from the sound-archive was the recording of that whistle.

Strangely enough, it was not this request which proved most difficult to satisfy.

NOËL, NOËL

That one sound is different.

So many sounds at this time of year. I have noted twenty-seven. That of Father's footstep before he opens the front door. Lighter as the holiday nears. His stair-step, dragging when it's been a long day. That of his slippers, the furry scuff towards the tinkle of the whisky decanter, and then the slosh in the glass. Mother's gait: quick in the dark of the morning, changing, a touch heavier after lights-on. The drum-roll of her heels, in and out. And that queer weightlessness, the pent-up breath of her first step before she enters the bedroom. I won't try and list the child-music. The scamper, right to the blown tip of her hair, when off to school. The skip at the gate. She dances to herself, at times, in her room. Tap and turn. Her laughters. Stuff my ears and I can still tell you of seven sorts. They ripple across one's skin.

There are, of course, the sayings of the house. When the heating clanks on or the rain dribbles. The flushings, the wince and quease (how would *you* put it?) of the stair-well. More door-voices than there are registers of wind. Warmth has its sound when it slides under the kitchen door. I know them all. They prickle my scalp. But this one is different.

I may be in error. Exceeding care is in order. Like that of the rat-catcher, arched and knit to hear the faintest creak, the cut whisper in the roof-beam or trestle. Error would be unforgivable. Come Christmas, sounds mix and multiply. And are shot through with smells. The shiver of the dwarf-pine with its green smell and hiss of needles; that of the post lurching through the slot in the door, heavier now with the waxen sound and scent of the glossy brochures and

91

catalogues; the crackle of wrappings and the whole house chiming, like the chandelier. Even the lone light in the attic sounds crystal gay. But here I must be prudent. Not only the candles in the window and on the mantelpiece give off a savour of felt and old copper; so do the electric bulbs, hung with pine-cones and holly, and on so much longer during these short days. One inhales sound and smell at one breath. Confusions may arise. (Days too soon I muddled the tide and ebb of voices from the school-yard – Penny does not have far to go in the morning, 'Not far to drop,' says Father, at which she pretends to flinch – with that of the carollers.) One cannot be too precise. I may be in error.

Yet that sound *is* different.

When did I first hear it?

I don't remember exactly. Not exactly, that is. To which uncertainty blame attaches. Is my memory weakening? It has been formidable. Not a whistling in the street or in the house that I ever forgot or confused with any other. Last spring's early thrush, the show-off, crochet-semi-quaver-crochet and the *rubato* on the trill. Ask me when Father bought the new wellies, the lined ones, or Mother burned the roast with the guests – I caught Mr Blakemore's rancid breath, those dentures, even before he banged the door-knocker – with the guests (did I already say that?) at the front steps. Ask me about Penny's mumps and their hot smell in the room, and the time (it was years ago, wasn't it?) when I heard her at the top of the landing, without slippers, passing her fingers and then her braids through the moonbeams, trying to count them one two three, sing-song, in her nightdress. With its odour of camphor, meaning start of school and leaves falling. Ask me. I will call up memory. How, then, is it that I don't recall, not exactly, the first time I heard the sound?

Could it have been when Mother was looking after her aunt – bronchial flu, was it? – and was away for the weekend? There are such sharp holes in the air when she is out of the house. Father and Penny had been to the movies. Four steps on the gravel. But then only two and the key fumbling in the lock. Because he was carrying her into the house, skipping, laughing. Penny was laughing too. And there were chocolate éclairs for tea, which Mother thinks bad for our teeth. So I was sworn to secrecy. 'Hi-ho the gang,' said Father and put rum in the tea. Only a drop for Penny and, at first, she wrinkled her nose and wouldn't. But then she sipped and coughed and giggled. The taste hung on our breath like warm gold. After which Father put on his favourite cassette, the *Pirates of Penzance* highlights, and he danced his hornpipe and knocked over the delphinia. So we were sworn to secrecy again and had raisin slices on top of the éclairs. Do you know what he did then? Put the raisins and bits of walnut to the edge of his lips and blew them out, in a high arc, telling Penny to catch them in her mouth. But they fell on the carpet and I was quicker. 'O Daddy, Daddy-O,' hummed Penny, spluttering and rounding her mouth. 'Daddy's duck,' he said. And she asked again when Mother would be back and why Auntie May had no one else to look after her, and couldn't Mum come home tonight. 'She would smell the chocolate éclairs,' said Father, *basso profundo*, and we would be in serious trouble, '*mucho* serious, Ducky.' Which made Penny giggle more.

Could it have been that night I first heard that sound?

Or was it at Nubb's Point?

I do detest picnics. Those ants; drawing-pins in my ears. But could it have been there? Consider the broad daylight. The herd of people about, squealing, snoring, licking wax-paper, huffing at one another, flying kites and screeching after them. Consider the loud slap of the lake against the piling. And the transistors. In all that squelch and flailing one can scarcely hear oneself sleep. True, there is the tunnel of shadow and of mildew behind the boathouse; and that odd thick spread of high grass and scrub downwind, away from the benches and the ices. But even there children swarm and couples cling (why else do they go on a picnic?). So it could not have been there, the sound I mean. Or could it? The time we dozed till twilight, till the early chill came off the water and Mother got up shivery. To pack the hampers, to shake the sand and dead grass out of the bath towels. Which was just when Father looped the beach-ball high and challenged Penny and me to the chase; beating us to its first bounce and punching it up again with his fist so that it arched into the late light and over the tea-stand. Where I lost them. There was muck in my eyes. I could hear them racing, breathing loud, and laughing. 'Penny for your thoughts, sweets for a penny,' Father's voice sliding away. I don't think it was then. And how could it have been, with Mother calling and starting towards the car-park? Revving motors and klaxons confuse me, like the yawp of gulls. I did say that I loathe picnics and the candy-drops underfoot.

What sound?

I find myself asking. Asking myself. Which is a muddle. Have I been imagining it, as I might certain smells? Does fear really have that scent of sodden cardboard? Is it in my head? I have seen old men tweeze out their hearing-aids and shake them bitterly, forgetting that the bat's piping is inside their skulls. It could just be, you know. I don't claim to be as sharp as I used to be. Other sounds, yes: twangings after the heavy winds, scratches as from somewhere behind my teeth, trills when I'm very thirsty. I might muddle or imagine those. But not that sound. It is too . . . Too what? I do have an especial

ear. Too *other*. I don't know that that makes sense. *Other*. Like
nothing else in earth or air. And there might just be something
in the word *other* which is like the shape and shadow of the
sound. The 'O' at the outset, the soft thud and the rasp. I can't
have imagined that soft scratching, like a hand through stubble. Night-beings, they say, move to that sound. Broken bits of
us loosed to the air when the moon is down.

But does it matter? I mean, does it matter where when I first
heard their sound? I am hearing it now. *Now*.

What a day it has been. The house caught in a bright wash
of bells. The door-bell: deliveries. A registered parcel – the
annual smoked ham from Father's cousin in York. Bells
pealing on the radio and at Evensong, on the box, out of some
vaulted nave, and those white voices of little boys chiming
Latin. 'Bluebells, tinklebells, twinklebells, Santa's a-coming.'
And the bird in the oven, crisping, crackling, simmering like
handbells in the far wood. If only the house wouldn't ring so.
It makes it hard to be certain. The door being shut.

Daddy dancing the evening long. Not literally, to be sure.
But walking, turning, standing as if always on his toes. Taking
the stairs at a bound. Whistling away the whisky on his breath.
Not leaving me be for even a minute. Calling, rubbing his hot
cheeks against mine. 'Old King Cole,' off-tune, incessant,
making the sitting-room rock. That 'merry old soul!' over and
over and over and Daddy-O slurping at me: 'Merry! Do you
hear me, you sad brute, merry! That ole King Cole, a goner,
high, on the trip of his boozy life. Jinglebells, *mon ami*. Heading
for our chimney. Merry! The soul of him bursting like grilled
sausage. You don't understand, do you, *mon ami*, with your
sad old eyes.' I do hate it when he speaks to me in French.
Dancing. I tell you the man was treading air. And those
stage-whispers: 'No peeking, Katkins. Off with you. Upstairs,

Penny and I have business. Wrappings to wrap. Ribbons to tie. For a certain special little lady. Off with you. I'll keep a weather-eye on the oven. Not to worry. For all manner of things shall be well. But nooo peeking, Slyboots. Not till tomorrow morning. Mummy's Christmas. Mummy's own very special Christmas. Right, Penny?' And Father swung Mother around the settee as if she were a child. I heard the light switch clicking off as she went upstairs. But the darkness wasn't dark. You understand, don't you? It pulsed, somehow. There was no stillness in the silence. After he and Penny had trimmed the tree, I mean, and put out Mummy's gifts, the chintz house-coat, the acacia plant, the toiletries in their starry mantles and tinsel. The darkness just wouldn't go quiet. You do know what I mean, *please*.

The thread of light under Penny's door. Pencil-thin and dark pink as is the shade on her bed-lamp. At first I couldn't make out the tune, the little old record-player which they rescued for Penny out of the attic last spring being so low. Then I caught the lilt of it. The *Snow White* medley. 'Whistle While You Work'. A favourite of hers. And somewhere somehow out of that soft piping, out of the filament of light under that door, came the sound, the oh-ing, so faint I could barely pick it up, the Daddy-O O-Daddy-waddy and the scudding breath, as through his mouth, the soft soft laughter, but more like a slipping out of key, sideways, out of true, the sound that is other. That is on the other side. Of what? I don't really know. On the other side of what can be borne. 'A penny for the guy. And mum's the word. Mum.' And this time the glassiness was out of his laughter. It was everyday. As if morning had come and the time for gifts. But it hasn't. Not yet.

My hind-legs ache. Badly. I am not as strong as I once was. But strong enough, still. When he opens the door – I love him so – I'll go for his throat. He is wearing his flannel house-shirt.

The plaid one, with the broken collar button. I shall aim for his throat. And the sound will cease. I have no choice. You do see that, don't you? It being Christmas.

A CONVERSATION PIECE

A humming as of bees, distant.

'But the Master, Eleazer son of Eleazer, in his commentary of 1611 said –'

'That Akhiba, may his name shine in glory, had been mistaken –'

'When he wrote that Abraham was altogether free, a man at liberty, the father of freedoms, when God, blessed be His unspeakable Name, called upon him to take the boy, Isaac, to the place of burnt offering.'

'By which Akhiba meant to signify that God's commandments are spoken to the spirit of man when that spirit is in a state of sovereignty over its own truth, that commandments to the enslaved and the maddened are empty.

'To which Eleazer son of Eleazer, he of Cracow, retorted –'

'"What freedom has man in the face of the summons of the Almighty?" When He commands, our freedom is obedience. Only the servant of God, the absolute servant, is a free man.'

'"Not so," said Baruch to me, he of Vilna. "Not so. When God bade Abraham, our father, take Isaac, his only son, to Mount Moriah, He paused for an answer. Abraham could have said: 'No'. He could have said: 'Almighty God, hallowed be Thy Name. You are tempting me. You are putting in my path the supreme temptation, which is unthinking, blind obedience. Such is the obeisance demanded by the Dragon Baal, by the empty gods with dog-heads in Egypt's temples. You are not Moloch, eater of children. What you now await from me is loving denial.'" So Baruch, my teacher.'

'The journey to the mountain took three days. During which Abraham did not speak to Isaac –'

'Nor to God. Who listened closely. Hoping for the answer

"No". Whose patience was without end and who was saddened. So Baruch, in our *schul* at Vilna, where the almond tree – '

'That's crazy. God's foreknowing is total. What need had He to listen to Abraham. He knew that His commandment would be obeyed, that it was not for man to question. I knew Baruch, your teacher. He was so subtle that in his hands words turned to sand.'

'Yet God, blessed be the hem of His unsayable Name and the fire-garment of His glory, did not wholly trust Abraham.'

'Another madman.'

'No. Listen to me. God's confidence in Abraham was not total. Let me hammer out my meaning. Do not interrupt. If God had been utterly certain that Abraham would strike down the boy, He would have let the sacrifice come to pass. And brought Isaac back to life. For is it not said that God can waken the dead? By putting the ram in the thicket, by saving the child, He left uncertain the final obedience of Abraham. Did not Gamaliel the Kabbalist instruct us that there are moments, openings in the universe, during which God questions His own foreknowledge, during which the Angel of the Unknown, of the nameless, passes across the light of being?'

'Gamaliel the heretic. The witch and alchemist of Toledo – '
Many voices now, close-crowded.

'That accounts for the gloss – '

'Gloss? What gloss, chatterbox?'

'In the Talmud in the *yeshivah*. Written in by hand.'

'Which *yeshivah*?'

'Ours. At Bialik. Saying that Abraham was angry. That anger choked him all the way home. That he did not speak once from Mount Moriah back to Beersheba.'

'*Angry*? Our father, Abraham, to whom God had restored Isaac?'

'Because the Almighty had not kept faith in him. Because God had not been absolutely certain that Abraham would fulfil His commandment and strike the knife into the boy. In the night after he had heard God's voice, and during the unendurable march to the mountain, Abraham had died many deaths. His senses had frozen. His brain had become like black dust. The heart had stopped its song. There was no ground under his feet, no dawn under his eyelids. His steps were like those of a bullock when it has been stunned, when the blood is already out of its throat. Those who looked on Abraham saw death walking. The faith in him had grown so mighty, the sinews of obedience so stretched, that there was no room for life. There was doubt in Moses, sanctified be his great name and remembrance. Mutiny in Jeremiah. But Abraham, he the father of our fathers, had been made faith. All else had been purged. He was faith in bone and nerve. No hair, no hair of a hair on him or in his unkempt beard but had become faith and obedience harder than steel. The knife was softer than his hand. The blade might snap. That was Abraham's last fear. But God did not know this. He did not choose to know it. His trust in Abraham, His servant, fell short. Now the Almighty would never have proof of Abraham's infinite faith. He would never know how tight was the knot of Abraham's obedience. As life came back into the old man, as pain came home to him, so did a towering anger. That, said the gloss, is why the silence on Abraham's return journey was more terrible than the silence on the road to Moriah.'

'Error. A false gloss. For has not Jehoshuah of Prague cleared up the matter of the silence? Has he not instructed us –'

'That Abraham's anger was the very opposite. He could not at first, and may he be forgiven, find it in his heart to praise, to thank God for the saving of Isaac. The terror had been too sharp. The temptation too severe for a man to bear. Unendurable because twofold. The temptation to obey was murderous and beyond human understanding. How could God ask such a thing of Abraham, his most faithful servant? The temptation to disobey. But is there anything worse than to deny God's voice, to close one's ears against His calling? That the Almighty had saved the child did not take away even an atom, an atom's breath of terror from His commandment and the three days thereafter. And what if God *had* taken Isaac? What if Abraham's knife had struck? What then? How could the boy's resurrection make up for his sacrifice, for Abraham's act of slaughter? On the way back to Beersheba, Abraham could not speak to God. The hurt, the doubts gagged his soul. Had not the ram appeared too late in the thicket? How could Abraham live after that moment on the mountain, how could Abraham draw breath after he had carried inside him the slaying of his son? Hence the grey sweat on him during the return, hence the total silence. So Jehoshuah, whom they stoned in Prague.'

For an instant the voices dropped. But then, like a grape bursting –

'Foolishness. Foolishness. Hair-splitting.'

Almost in chorus.

'God had promised Abraham "I will make of thee a great nation". He had promised father Abraham that his seed would be as are the stars, numberless, inextinguishable even when scattered. He had renewed with Abraham the covenant of hope. That Israel would endure, that Abraham's seed would be sown across the earth. Indestructible as is the living wind.'

'That it would endure despite –

'The destruction of the temple and the loss of Zion –

'Despite massacre and dispersal –

'That we should not be consumed, not finally, in the fiery furnace, in the teeth of the mob, in the charnel house or the pogrom –

'That we shall endure even after they have torn the almond tree from its roots –

'Like hot ashes through the night. Alive even in death. Alive.

'"A nation and a company of nations shall be of thee," said God to our fathers, despite –

'But how then could Abraham have believed, even for a minute, that the Almighty, sung be His Name of Names, would have him slay Isaac? For without Isaac there could be no lineage, no children of Israel? Answer me that.'

'Was it all a game? Play-acting, as at *Purim*? When Haman roars through his black beard that all Jews, both young and old, little children and women, shall perish in one day, and the spoil shall be taken from them for a prey? O, that black roaring. How it frightens us, how the children in the hall hold their breath and crowd close to their parents. Though we know that Esther is in the wings and that evil Haman will hang high. God and Abraham acting out the play of Isaac. To make our hearts breathless. To teach us by terror and by joy, as children must be taught. And Abraham was silent because he knew that all would be well, that he would, through Isaac, be a father to nations. Silent as was Joseph when he recognized his brethren and looked on Benjamin.'

'But where then would be Abraham's merit? Play-acting? When the being of God is, as Maimonides taught, truth. A truth so pure that there is no shadow, no shadow of a shadow where it prevails. Abraham was an old man, a very old man – '

'Who might have forgotten then, in the numbness of that terrible calling, the terms of God's promise, so long ago, in the land of Ur – '

'Who might have thought, in the dizziness of his fear, that God would bring to Sarah another son, a child of late evening after Isaac – '

'Who could have believed that the Lord, blessed be His Name, had changed purpose, that some other people, and not Israel, would be sanctified among nations. Because even Abraham, father of our fathers, had known sin, being a man. Or so it is argued in the commentary of the learned Ephraim of Mainz. I remember the passage.'

'And for all these reasons, or others we are too blind, too unlettered to apprehend, Abraham might have taken for the voice of God that of a demon – '

'That of Satan himself.'

'Abraham in his numbness, in his dizziness, in his knowledge of imperfection, mistaking the whisper of Satan for the voice of God. For was it not said by Soloviel the Kabbalist that these two voices, that of God whom we must not name and that of un-nameable evil, are so utterly alike. That the difference between them is only that of the sound of a rain-drop in the sea?'

'It *was* the voice of Satan. God is no play-actor. Neither is *he* a sadistic tempter. How do we best define God, how do we seek to imagine Him? Precisely as one who *cannot* ask of a man that he stick a knife in the throat of his child. There is no surer proof that God is than the incapacity of our souls, of our minds, to conceive of Him as tempting Abraham to murder his son, to conceive of Him as torturing Abraham our father during the journey to the mount. Even a gentile, albeit the wisest among them, understood that the definition, the being of God, is proved by the impossibility of the commandment to Abraham. That it was Satan who confounded Abraham and seduced him to his devilish purpose.'

'A gentile? What gentile?'

'He bore a name like ours: Immanuel. He lived in Koenigsberg.'

'In Koenigsberg? I have a cousin there. Menachem the draper. Do you know him, the shop in the old town square? Do you know what has happened –'

'And having observed the confusion of Abraham, the Almighty betook Himself to Mount Moriah, set an angel to guard Isaac and wove the ram into the thorn-bush. Perhaps the selfsame bush that would burn for Moses.'

'Why then, *rebbi*, did God not intervene at once? Why did he not drive Satan from Abraham's door and take the old man out of his agony? The journey took three whole days. Three long nights Abraham lay awake with the face of Isaac before him, with that knife in his belt. An eternity. Why?'

'Our time is not His. Perhaps that ram was not yet born or the bush thick enough. Perhaps in His infinite mercy, the Almighty, praised be He, sought to give Satan a chance, to see whether the Fallen One would feel remorse seeing the sweat on Abraham, and undo his evil trick.'

'Though you are a learned man, you speak like a simpleton. You say that we know the being of God, the meaning of Him, just because He could not order Abraham to sacrifice Isaac the child, the only son. You would have us believe that so crazy, so obscene a commandment could come only from Satan. God's existence tells us that Abraham was mistaken when he took the voice of the devil for that of the Lord. You cite a wise man of the gentiles. Perhaps he was wise. But no true Christian. For is the God of the Christians not He who gives His only son in sacrifice, who let His son die in bestial pain on the Roman cross?'

A rush of voices.

'But that is not our God. Not ours. Not –'

'Our God is one. He does not beget. All men are His sons. The Nazarite was no Messiah. Only a man. Mad, perhaps.'

'Let me speak. I do not say that their God is ours, or that Christ was His child. I can attach no meaning to such words. But consider this: only Almighty God, only He who spoke to Job out of the whirlwind and slew the first-born of Egypt, could command Abraham to sacrifice Isaac. Abraham was not mistaken. His hearing was good. Listening to those terrible words, words which should never cross the lips of the living, Abraham *knew* that God was speaking. God is what He is because He alone can demand of His most faithful servant that he slit his child's throat. And it was this knowledge, this understanding beyond reason, which made father Abraham speechless on the journey to the mountain and mute on the road back to Beersheba. We who are fallen into the hand of the living God –'

Was the sound nearing? A sound slithering, like smoke across sand.

Next, a voice lime-green and acid.

'Who speaks for Isaac?'

Not yet a man's voice. Choked by the first starched collar and the bite of the collar-stud.

'Who speaks for Isaac? It was a hard march. His father Abraham walking too fast. Saying nothing, but pulling him by the hand. Black, impatient as Isaac had never seen his father before, but silent. Isaac saw the dry wood and the flint. He knew that his father was carrying a knife and a whetstone. But where was the lamb for the burnt offering? And when he asked, his father said that God would provide. But the words sounded strange, like the beads of sweat on Abraham's lips. Do you think Isaac believed him? I don't. He must have guessed. From the way in which they hurried from the house, from the way they camped in the night, hardly washing, all under one stinking tent-cloth. Oh, Isaac must have guessed and smelled the knife. And fouled himself in his fear. Marching three days with his bowels cold and loose, trying to sleep three short nights in the stench of his fear. Can you imagine their climb up the mountain? It may be that Abraham carried the wood, giving to Isaac the flint and shavings for the fire. But Isaac must have noticed the rope around the logs. Too thick, too freshly woven. A rope with which to tie a man's hands behind his back. Why did he not scream for help or run back to the young servants whom Abraham had left at the foot of the trail? Isaac's friends. The serving-men with whom he played in the court-yard of the house, who brought him the new grapes from the vine and cut arrows for him? Surely they would hide him and spirit him home. Why did Isaac not seize his father's hands and cry out for his life? Why did he not snatch at the knife and throw it over the side of the hill?'

'Because the spirit of God was upon him, because he was blessed in obedience.'

'Because Abraham's ass, the brindled she-ass whom Isaac fed, had whispered to him that he need not fear, that an Angel was beside him. There is a *midrasch* which says that the beast of burden spoke comfort to Isaac.'

'Fairy-tales. Lies. I will tell you why Isaac did not scream for help or run away or try to stop his father. It was because he was too frightened. It was because his voice had frozen inside him. It was because he was ashamed of the hot dirt and smell in his pants. The shame being even greater than his fear of death. But when Abraham bound him and laid him out on the altar, on that dry, sharp wood, when he heard the knife come out of his father's belt, he screamed. No one heard that scream. Because Isaac was vomiting, because the vomit was in his mouth, like a gag. But I know that he screamed.'

'Nowhere in the Torah, nowhere in the scrolls of truth – '

'But I hear the scream,' said the boy. 'All around me. And inside my head. Since we left for the station. It is Isaac's scream, which has never ceased.'

Refutation is made. But gently.

'You must be mistaken, boy. There was no scream. And even if there had been, it stopped at once. The Angel called out. And Isaac's heart leaped and sang at the great blessing: "I will multiply thy seed as the stars of the heaven, and as the sand which is upon the sea shore; and thy seed shall possess the gate of his enemies." And when they came home to Beersheba, they feasted and rejoiced in the Lord. The ass was put to pasture and Isaac the child was given the ram's horn, circled with gold, to blow on. It is that horn you hear, calling to the hills.'

'I don't believe you.' Even shriller. 'I don't believe you. I can't. It's like the sweets they cram in your mouth after you've had a tooth pulled. Do you know what those sweets taste like? You don't, do you! Of blood and pus.'

'But Isaac loved Abraham. His love never wavered. It was Abraham his father who chose Rebekah for him. And when Abraham died at 165 years of age, his blessing was on Isaac and Isaac tore his hair in grief.'

'Bedtime stories. No man lives that long. Isaac never trusted Abraham again. Not for one instant. How could he? How could he forget the walk to Moriah, the faggots, the rope, the knife? The taste of his father's hand on his eyes and mouth, of Abraham's knee in his back, never left him. That is why Isaac was deceived by *his* sons, by Esau and Jacob. No Jewish father looks on his son without remembering that he may be commanded to take back his life. No Jewish son looks on his father without remembering that he may be sacrificed by his father's hand. How can there be trust or forgiveness between us? Blood and pus. Don't you smell it, you who call yourselves teachers, masters of the word?'

The young voice skidded, like a cracked pipe, soon inaudible. In the droning dark.

'And what of Sarah?'

A woman speaking. An angry chorus.

'Silence. Silence. Is it not ordained by the Law that no woman shall come to the Torah? That women, though blessed and honoured is their mystery, shall not comment on holy writ?'

'Then why are we here, behind the same closed door? You have never given us a sabbatical from pain. Never a leave of absence from massacre. Though you would have us be silent, we are branded like you. Sarah *knew*. How could she not have known? How can any mother not know when her child is taken from her to be slaughtered? Old Abraham told her to be silent, to stay out of God's unfathomable way. But she saw the wood, the rope, the knife. She smelled the cold fear in the old man's groin and the hot fear in the boy's hair. They stole away before sun-up, like foxes from the hen-house. But she was awake. She heard their lying steps on the threshold and the drowsy coughs of the serving-men. She lay awake, did Sarah, crazed with fear, her guts turning to stone. Six nights and six days, her eyes so hot with horror

111

that she could no longer weep. And when they came back from the mountain, the men and the boy – her child, her only son – they told her to prepare a great feast, to deck the great table with fresh green, to send for flute-players and dancers from Ashod. When all she wanted was to hold the child, so close he would feel the fire in her bones, and cry out her pain. During those six days and nights, Sarah's whole life had passed before her. How Abraham had handed her over to Abimelech, king of Gerar, how he had handed her over for the king to whore with, lying to save his own precious hide, saying "she is my sister". How other women had laughed at her, behind their fluttering hands, when she became pregnant with Isaac, how no one believed that the old frozen man was Isaac's father – did Abraham himself believe it? Sarah saw before her the years during which she had had to endure in her house, in her kitchen, in the vegetable garden, Hagar the Egyptian and the dark son she had borne Abraham, how she had had to endure the scent of burnt almonds from Hagar's skin, Abraham's scent. And even as she lay dying, Sarah heard, in Abraham's train, the chirping of women, of the concubines that came with him to Hebron. Do you really think she did not know, in her parched hollowness, that Abraham would, immediately after her death, take to wife Keturah, the girl with the good teeth? But what did it matter, what did anything matter after those days of Mount Moriah, after this boy's footsteps had been taken from the house? What could make up for that? The Holy Books report nothing of Sarah's torture. No learned commentator reports what she felt when she heard the lick of the ass's hoofs on the cobbles but dared not look whether Isaac was among the men coming home. No man, no one who has not borne a child, can imagine that. We women are not called up to read the Torah. A good thing for you. It is between the lines we would be reading, between every two lines. For in that space lies the silence of women. Who have had no say among you. It is the loudest silence in the world. Loud with the cries of labour and with the cries of all the mothers who have seen their children beaten to death in front of their eyes. But now you must hear it, you men. In this meeting-house we no longer sit and pray apart from you. Here we also are called, we daughters of silence.'

Another woman's voice, and a third: 'Dance, Miriam, dance. In this small house – '

Too small, really. Not a dancing-floor at all. Not that it terribly mattered. Men and women, oh, impropriety, young and old, were now welded so close that the merest motion, a raw breath out of a single mouth, quivered through the lot.

'A thousand years you men have argued, ravelled, spun words. You have read yourselves blind, crooked your backs, poring over the single letter or the missing vowel. A thousand years you have chanted and swayed as if truth could be caught in your fingers. You have burrowed for meaning like starved mice and pounded the words so fine they have fallen to dust. Living men, their lips caked with dust, as are the buried. You have hissed and croaked at one another, owls at noon-time. We have heard you when we passed the closed shutters of the schools, we have heard you when you lay beside us in the night, expostulators, litigants, cross-examiners, word-peddlers even in your dreams. To what end? Have you found those syllables which make up the secret name of God? What pun, what game of hidden numbers has made us free? Was it all for *this*?'

'Thought is the dance of the mind. The spirit dances when it seeks out meaning, and the meaning of that meaning. Perhaps there is in the forty-ninth letter of the forty-ninth verse of the forty-ninth chapter of the Book of Books, which

113

lies hidden in the Torah as the Torah rolls lie cloaked inside their shrine, a truth so mighty that God Himself must pause when He remembers it. The dance-steps of the soul are words, woman. The lords of the dance are we. Are we not dancing now?'

Up steps of air.

Which grew steeper and steeper.

Mountainous. Higher than Moriah.

'Dance, Miriam, dance,' said the spigot in the ceiling.

'There is no ram now and the bush is burning.'

Dancers, their mouths wide open. So that the hive swarmed into their throats. And hummed to them the slurred slow song of ash.